SWANS & KLONS

Visit us at www.boldstrokesbooks.com

SWANS & KLONS

by

Nora Olsen

2013

ISBN 10: 1-60282-874-1
ISBN 13: 978-1-60282-874-2

This Trade Paperback Original Is Published By
Bold Strokes Books, Inc.
P.O. Box 249
Valley Falls, NY 12185

First Edition: May 2013

CREDITS
EDITOR: RUTH STERNGLANTZ
PRODUCTION DESIGN: SUSAN RAMUNDO
COVER DESIGN BY SHERI (GRAPHICARTIST2020@HOTMAIL.COM)

Acknowledgments

Thanks to the amazing Lev Olsen, Sondra Spatt Olsen, and Ara Hale Burklund, who took the time to read the manuscript and gave me great feedback. Thanks to Crystal Malarsky Laffan, as well as Mark Eastburn and the other writers in our March 2010 SCBWI NJ conference critique group. And thanks to Frances Hogg Lochow, Brian Higley, Simon Verkhovsky, Alpha S., Anita Merando, and Olive for reading many chapters in our old writers group.

Thanks to everyone at Bold Strokes Books, especially: my terrific editor, Ruth Sternglantz; Radclyffe, for bringing me into the family; Cindy Cresap, Sandy Lowe, Connie Ward, and Kim Baldwin for all your help.

Thanks also to Kelly Kingman for helping me with my query letter, Chris Prestia for your excellent advice, and Steve Berman. Rebecca Dingler, and Amy Estrada for being great 2009 NaNoWriMo MLs in the Poughkeepsie region, and Chris Baty for inventing National Novel Writing Month in the first place. Thanks to Daniel Rutter of http://www.howtospotapsychopath.com and commenter corinoco for your inspiring online discussion of airships.

Thanks to writers Nicola Griffith, Lois McMaster Bujold, and Jane Fletcher —you light the way for the rest of us. And to Adam Rex for these profound words from *The True Meaning of Smekday*, "Everybodies always is wanting to make a clone for to doing their work. If you are not wanting to do your work, why would a clone of you want to do your work?"

Above all, thanks to Áine Ní Cheallaigh, the best girlfriend anyone could ever dream of.

Dedication

For my mother, Sondra Spatt Olsen

CHAPTER ONE

She knew it was childish, but sometimes Rubric still wanted to spend time with her Nanny Klon. She stood in Nanny Klon's windowless room in Yellow Dorm, waiting for her to get back. The bed was folded into the wall, so there wasn't even a place to sit down.

A drawer that wasn't closed all the way caught Rubric's eye. Her Jeepie Type was well known for being obsessed with order and symmetry. She tried to close it and found a flat, crinkly object sticking out. It felt almost like a leaf, but it looked like something woman-made. Then she saw writing on it and realized it was a piece of paper, like from the olden days.

Rubric found everything about historic times rather disgusting. She tried to appreciate ancient literature by Brontë and Rowling and people like that, but she couldn't stop thinking about the fact that all those people used to have fetuses inside their bodies—*pregnancies*—and then *gave birth*. Gross, gross, gross! Also she found it hard to relate to the male characters—the *men*.

She examined the writing scrawled across the piece of paper. She had never known that Klons were capable of reading. But there was no reason they shouldn't be. Klons weren't thicko, they just weren't human.

The paper read:

Dear Bloom,

I don't know when I will ever see you again. Try your best to write back. The Milk Delivery Klon said she doesn't mind carrying messages. I miss you so much, but I'm trying to pay attention to my new assignment.

She skipped to the bottom:

My love forever,
Shine

She folded it and put it back. The drawer was crammed with other papers. Rubric wondered why Nanny Klon was saving these people's messages. Just as she shut the drawer carefully, Nanny Klon returned.

"Rubric, my pet!" Nanny Klon opened her big arms and Rubric went in for a hug. Nanny Klon had once told Rubric that she had to drink a flagon of fat with each meal and one at bedtime to keep her body at the optimal level of soft and comforting, because Nanny Klon's Jeepie Type tended toward thinness. The Doctors believed that teenagers responded better to Nanny Klons who were plump. When Rubric was younger, she used to buy peppermint oil for Nanny Klon to make her flagons of fat taste more palatable, but she hadn't thought of such a thing in a long time.

"Now, how's that schatzie of yours?" Nanny Klon asked, releasing her.

"Salmon Jo's fine," Rubric said.

Nanny Klon sighed. "First love," she said. "I've seen so many girls falling in love for the first time while they were living in Yellow Dorm. Now, I know you didn't just come here to say hello to me. What's on your mind?"

"Tomorrow's the day we're going to be matched with our Jeepie Similar mentors," Rubric told her. "I'm really worried about who I'm going to get."

"You'll be paired with someone very creative," Nanny Klon said. "Just like you."

"Yeah, I know that," Rubric said. "But I wonder who, specifically. I've been looking up people in the city for months, looking for people who look like my Jeepie Similars. And there's this artist. Her name is Stencil Pavlina. Have you heard of her?"

Nanny Klon shook her head. Rubric wasn't surprised. Klons didn't know about art or anything else that was really important.

"The first time I ever saw pictures of her sculptures, I felt a special connection with them," Rubric said. "Then we saw some of them in person on the annual trip, and I felt it even more. I was almost jealous, like, why didn't *I* make them? So I always wondered if she was the same Jeepie Type as me. I looked her up, and she looks just like me, only old."

"She sounds nice, dear," Nanny Klon said. "But don't get your hopes up too much. I'm sure whoever they pick will be just right for you."

"Does that really always happen?" Rubric asked. "You've seen lots of girls get matched when they turned sixteen."

"They always get the right mentor," Nanny Klon said.

That wasn't really the same as getting the mentor you want, Rubric thought.

"Okay, thanks," she said, even though Nanny Klon had been no help. As a little child she had been trained to be polite to the Klons. *Just because they're not human is no reason they shouldn't be treated with respect*, she had been lectured.

"I can understand why you're nervous," Nanny Klon said. "This is a big moment in your life. You're growing up—why, you're almost a Panna, not a child anymore! What about Salmon Jo? Is she hoping for someone specific?"

"Of course," Rubric said. "Not a specific person, but she wants to be matched with a scientist who's studying Cretinous Males from the olden days. You know how she is—she's dead set on it."

"Her Jeepie Type sometimes has trouble being matched with a mentor."

"I never heard that," Rubric said. "What makes you think so?"

"I've seen so many girls over the years in Yellow Dorm. Her Jeepie Type is complicated. They have a hard time with certain things."

Rubric was surprised Nanny Klon would tell her this. "What kind of things?"

"Oh, that won't happen to Salmon Jo," Nanny Klon said. "She has a good head on her shoulders. And she has you to look out for her!"

"I definitely keep Salmon Jo out of trouble," Rubric said. "Oh, I almost forgot. There was something that looked like… paper? in one of your drawers."

An expression Rubric couldn't classify passed quickly across Nanny Klon's face.

"Who are Bloom and Shine?" Rubric asked. "Why do you have their messages?"

Nanny Klon smiled gently. "Is that all? Why, I'm Bloom."

"What do you mean?"

"We Klons have names too. So we can tell each other apart. There are lots of Nanny Klons in this city, even just in this academy. How would anyone know which one was me? And don't forget, when I was a child I wasn't a Nanny Klon yet."

Rubric never saw Klon children; they were kept at their own academies. "I never thought about that before," she said.

"You never asked before," Nanny Klon said. "Now, you run along. I bet Salmon Jo is pulsing you right now. You should be out enjoying yourself, not stuck with your boring, old Nanny Klon."

Rubric walked down the stairs, thinking about Klons having names. Some people gave individual names to their personal Klons, but Rubric had always thought it was kind of affected. Bloom and Shine were strange names. They were nouns, like a name should be, but they were also verbs, which was not normal.

Her handheld screen pulsed in the pocket of her tunic. It was Salmon Jo, asking her to meet at the VR arcade. Rubric left the dorm and cut across the lawn in front of the stately yellow-brick building that had been her home for four years. Girls always took this shortcut, and the grass had worn away. Everything about the campus—the seven dormitories, the centuries-old classroom buildings, the refectory, the ivy-covered library—was so familiar to her, that looking around gave her a tired feeling. She couldn't wait until she was matched with her mentor and allowed to leave campus and roam the city whenever she wanted.

A Gardener Klon had parked her tiny electric car by the main green and was pulling out rakes. Rubric realized something was still nagging her about her conversation with Nanny Klon. It wasn't until she had crossed the main green on the flagstone-tiled path that she figured it out. Nanny Klon hadn't entirely answered her question. Who was Shine?

The VR arcade was right behind the refectory where the girls ate all their meals. Rubric was startled to see so few people in the arcade. There were a few young kids at the driving game and the flying game. But there was no one waiting in line at *Who Shall Be My Schatzie? The Game.* That was only the best, most popular game ever. Then Rubric heard shouts and laughter, and she saw a crowd in the far corner where the boring educational games were. All the girls were clustered around one game, jostling each other to see. Had everyone gone veruckt?

As Rubric got closer, the situation began to make sense. There were about thirty girls pushing and shoving to see the display. The game was called Parade of Perfection, and it was supposed to teach you about notable women of every Jeepie Type, from the earliest days of Society through the present. Ordinarily, it would be stultifyingly dull. But not the day before you were matched with your Jeepie Similar mentor! Some clever girl had realized they could use this game to figure out who they might be matched with. Rubric grinned and shook her head. She got herself a frozen lemonade from the drinks dispenser and went to join the others.

Her friend Banner had the controls. Banner was tossing her head to get her wavy black hair out of her eyes. The display flashed dizzyingly through graphics of different Pannas who all looked kind of alike. It came to rest on one, a woman who resembled Banner but was older, sophisticated looking, and had glam black hair down to her knees.

"I bet she's the one!" Banner cried. "She lives in the city! Look, it says she has a pet leopard with a diamond collar!"

Rubric tapped Banner on the shoulder.

"Hey, Ru!" Banner said. "Guess what, that artist you keep talking about is in here!" She manipulated the controls and whizzed through the menus until she came to a graphic of Panna Stencil Pavlina, the sculptor Rubric was hoping would be her mentor. The older woman looked haughty and overbearing.

"This is what she looked like when she was in academy," Banner said, clicking on something. Another graphic leapt to the front, and Rubric caught her breath. Except for the fact that Stencil Pavlina was wearing the uniform tunic of a different academy and a hairstyle of yesteryear, it could have been a graphic of Rubric herself. Same tall, sturdy frame. Same straight brown hair, same open and direct gaze in her hazel eyes.

It made Rubric feel funny. She had always resented her ordinary and wholesome appearance. She wished she looked wan and temperamental. If only her Jeepie Type had pointy cheekbones and soulful coal-black eyes. But maybe Rubric would be able to change her appearance as much as Panna Stencil Pavlina had.

"My turn!" another girl said, pushing Banner out of the way and snatching the controls. The display flickered back to the top menu, and the music changed. "You've been hogging it long enough."

Rubric couldn't see her schatzie anywhere, but she saw her friend Filigree Sue. "Where's Salmon Jo?" Rubric asked her. It was so loud she had to shout.

"I'm not sure," Filigree Sue said, not flickering her gaze away from the game. "She went through that door."

Rubric fought her way back out of the crowd. She almost made it out unscathed, but at the last minute a girl knocked her drink onto the floor. Summoning the Klon behind the counter to clean up the mess, Rubric got another frozen lemonade and opened the door in the back.

It was the room where all the circuit breakers and electrical things were. Salmon Jo's toned runner's legs were dangling out of one of the ceiling panels.

Rubric went over and tickled her ankle.

"Aah!" Salmon Jo shrieked. More of her slowly emerged. She jumped down, all dusty. There was some kind of gray powder in her tightly curled dark hair. Her golden eyes shone with her usual enthusiasm. "*Mmm,* can I have some of that?"

Rubric surrendered her lemonade. "What're you doing up there?"

"It's kind of a tunnel. I want to see where it goes, but there are so many wires in the way that it's hard to maneuver."

"How can you be thinking about some tunnel at a time like this?"

"Everyone is freaking out over nothing, and acting thicko," Salmon Jo said. "I'm sure we're all going to get exactly who we want. Why shouldn't we?"

Her complacence was half reassuring, half annoying.

"You really think so?" Rubric asked.

"Of course. Would you give me a boost back up? I'll be real fast."

Rubric did, and Salmon Jo wriggled all the way up and disappeared. Suddenly, the cheerful music from the VR room stopped, and she heard a collective cry of dismay. Then the lights flickered out.

"Oops," said Salmon Jo from the ceiling.

CHAPTER TWO

Before she had started dating Salmon Jo, Rubric had thought there was only one problem with her life: she knew everyone. Sure, it was a close-knit community in the dorms and at the academy, but it was hard to find a schatzie. How could you get romantic about someone if you had known her since before puberty and remembered the time she threw up in the cafeteria, or how she used to pretend she was a pony? You just couldn't. Rubric had always wanted to meet a beautiful, brooding stranger. And it had finally happened. Sort of.

She had known who Salmon Jo was. But they had always lived in different dorms and moved in separate circles. Rubric respected her in an abstract way because Salmon Jo was well-known for being a science head. Of course, science was boring, but at least the girl cared about stuff other than parties, gossip, who was whose schatzie, and what the coolest clothes were. Beyond that, she never thought about Salmon Jo at all.

Until six months ago in the Sky Room. The Sky Room was Rubric's favorite place, even though it was just a small room on the top floor of the Rec Building. She liked it because it had so many windows and a huge skylight. Rubric liked to bring her handheld screen and draw there. It was rare for Rubric to have the room all to herself. It was funny to think now that she had actually been disappointed when Salmon Jo came in. Salmon Jo didn't bother her, though; she just took out her own screen and started reading.

Rubric was making up a graphic novel about an airship that traveled around the world, its people living happy and fulfilled lives. It was just like real Society, except the people had to keep everything they needed on the ship. She couldn't exactly come up with a plot, since she had made their lives perfect, so she was sketching the airship. She wanted it to be constructed of modern transluminum but to be powered like the zeppelins of the ancient past.

She had drawn two balloons filled with helium and was working on the engine, when Salmon Jo spoke.

"Excuse me, but I think you should house the engine cars outside the hull to reduce the chance that the hydrogen gets ignited by the exhaust flame or some kind of spark."

Rubric had never even seen Salmon Jo glance up from her screen, let alone examine the drawing. For that matter, Salmon Jo was barely looking at her now. Her eyes kept flitting away. "It's helium, not hydrogen," Rubric said. Why was this girl criticizing her drawing? That was totally veruckt!

Salmon Jo shrugged. "Either way. I think hydrogen would give you more lift, though."

Rubric realized the girl had understood exactly what she was drawing without having to be told. So it must be a pretty good picture. Rubric really didn't want to have to start all over, just to put the engine cars in a different place.

"Of course, I shouldn't just point out all the mistakes without saying what a mouthwateringly good drawing it is, but there is just one more thing. I mean it's really lovely—"

"Oh, just spit it out," Rubric said.

"The swimming pool. It's a bit unrealistic. A swimming pool must weigh hundreds of tons. It would be way too heavy."

"This is a huge ship. You can't see the scale from the drawing."

"It could be huge, but it still couldn't hold that much weight."

"I think it could," Rubric said. If the people were going to be happy, they obviously needed a swimming pool. She sniffed and turned away from Salmon Jo.

"This is just a question of fact," the girl persisted. "It's not a matter of opinion."

"There are no facts here," Rubric said. "This is an imaginary airship we're arguing about. I mean, the swimming pool is the least of your worries here when it comes to plausibility. But it's my imaginary ship so I'll have a swimming pool on it if I want to."

She was immediately embarrassed at her own childishness. She looked over at Salmon Jo and saw that she was biting her lip to keep from laughing. Then Salmon Jo snorted, appallingly loudly.

"I'm sorry," Salmon Jo said.

"Probably all the water would slosh out of the pool every time the airship made a hard turn," Rubric admitted. She noticed that since the last time she'd really looked at Salmon Jo, Salmon Jo had gotten a new haircut that made her short corkscrew curls look very cute. Salmon Jo had nice eyes, a golden color that reminded Rubric of agave nectar. Salmon Jo was shorter than Rubric, but her sinewy frame and abundance of energy made her seem tall.

"Actually, I have an idea for an airship too," Salmon Jo said. "Instead of hydrogen or helium, a vacuum would make it float. It would be shaped like a diatom."

"A what?" Rubric asked.

"It's a kind of phytoplankton," Salmon Jo explained. "The kind I'm thinking of is sort of in the shape of a ribbon. Very pretty."

Rubric wondered why she hadn't just said the ship would be shaped like a ribbon. Who thought about the shapes of phytoplankton? And thought they were pretty? Salmon Jo, apparently. Rubric was going to ask what a phytoplankton was but thought better of it.

"The ship would require elements and sheets with tensile strength," Salmon Jo said, warming to her subject. "Ideally, a frictionless material, which of course doesn't actually exist. My airship might implode, but it definitely wouldn't burn. So that would make a nice change from hydrogen."

"I don't understand a word you just said, except for *and* and *the*," Rubric said.

"Okay, well, if you think about the basic physics—"

"I never took physics," Rubric said. "I don't have time for that kind of tripe."

"You…never…took…physics," Salmon Jo said. "You're sixteen years old and you never took physics? You're one of those humanities girls. I don't believe it. I've never had an intelligent conversation before with a humanities girl."

"What makes you think you've ever had an intelligent conversation, period?" Rubric snapped.

Salmon Jo laughed, revealing neat white teeth.

"I'm going to narrow my focus to what we have in common," Salmon Jo said, touching Rubric's arm lightly. "We both like airships. And the idea of flying, in general?"

Rubric nodded. "Did you ever do the trick of levitating someone?" she found herself asking.

"Yeah, at a dorm party," Salmon Jo said.

"You want to try?" Rubric asked.

"I'm not sure if it will work with just us," Salmon Jo said. "I mean, you need a whole lot of people to create the illusion of—"

"*Sssh,*" Rubric said. "Turn off your science brain."

"Have you noticed you keep interrupting me?" Salmon Jo grumbled, but she lay down and wriggled a little closer to Rubric. Salmon Jo closed her eyes, and Rubric slipped her fingers under Salmon Jo's neck. Salmon Jo seemed tense at first, but then Rubric could feel her muscles relax.

"Light as a feather, stiff as a board," she intoned. Since Salmon Jo had her eyes closed, she could examine her face as much as she wanted. Her eyelids themselves were beautiful. Rubric was already imagining Salmon Jo as her future schatzie, even though they'd never kissed or been on a date.

Four or five giggling girls slammed into the room, but Salmon Jo didn't open her eyes. Rubric kept cradling her head in her hands. She was positive Salmon Jo liked her.

Chapter Three

The foyer outside the auditorium was jammed with girls, but Rubric's friends had pulsed her with instructions to meet them under the huge engraved Golden Rule on the wall. She found them by the big OTHERS in DO UNTO OTHERS AS YOU WANT THEM TO DO UNTO YOU. Salmon Jo kissed her distractedly, half on the lips and half on the cheek, and squeezed her hand. Rubric was immediately drawn into the excited chatter of her friends.

"Rubric, I know who my mentor will be," Banner insisted. "I can just feel it."

"That's ridiculous," Rubric scoffed, even though she felt the same way about Stencil Pavlina.

"My future mentor has the largest collection of shoes in the city," Banner said. "Maybe in all of Society. She's really glam!"

Rubric couldn't even count the number of times Banner had told her this. She also couldn't believe this was the last time they would have this conversation because in just a few minutes they would find out the truth.

"I think I just saw my future mentor in the "Cream Of Society" column," Filigree Sue said. "Look!" She brought up the article on her handheld screen and showed it to them.

Rubric could see that the beautifully coiffed Panna bore no resemblance to Filigree Sue. But she didn't want to burst her bubble.

Banner had no such qualms. "Good gravy!" she said. "You're turning into another Hollyhock!"

Hollyhock had lived in Maroon Dorm. About a year ago, she had started saying a lot of veruckt stuff, almost like hallucinations. And kind of vulgar. She was saying that she was in love with the Chef Klon in her dorm. Then Doctors had come to take her away because she needed a kidney transplant. Adults needed kidney transplants all the time, but kids didn't, usually. So that had been exciting because Rubric had never seen a Doctor in the flesh, except at her annual physical exam. It was cool to see the beautiful Doctor stride in, wearing her special saffron-colored robes, surrounded by a retinue of blue-robed Klons. Ever since then, her group of friends called you a Hollyhock if you were acting particularly veruckt.

"What do you mean?" asked Filigree Sue.

"There's no way that Panna is your Jeepie Similar, you thicko. She looks nothing like you. Look at her tiny upturned nose."

Filigree Sue put her hand to her nose. "I think she looks like me," she said in a muffled voice and glanced back at her screen.

Salmon Jo was staring at a screen too, but she was reading about Cretinous Males.

"I don't know who mine will be, but I'm going to have so much fun with her," said Concept. "She can show me what colors look best on me. And show me all around the city."

Rubric wondered what her friends would have to give their lives meaning. She had art and Salmon Jo had science. Maybe Banner, Concept, and Filigree Sue would be happy spending the rest of their lives watching edfotunement and doing their hair. That must be a quality of their Jeepie Types. She couldn't picture them as being among the tiny cohort of girls who were selected to be Doctors or to have careers.

"She'll take me to real parties! And all the spectacles!" Filigree Sue said. "Isn't it going to be amazing when we can leave campus any time we want? All the fifteen year olds are going to be on their pathetic annual trip off campus, all wearing the same color tunics and being herded by their teachers and Nanny Klons. And I'll be strolling along all alone, or maybe with my mentor. Sipping a chicory coffee."

Rubric tried to imagine herself walking around the city all alone but failed.

Salmon Jo looked up from her handheld screen. "Filigree, you always loved the annual trip."

"I did, but I'm so past it now. Did you find your scientist mentor?" Filigree Sue asked.

"I didn't waste my time on that," Salmon Jo said. "When I filled out the form, I explained that I wanted to be matched with someone who's working on the Cretinous Male issue. It's only the greatest unsolved mystery in all of history, why they became cretinous. I'm sure it took the teachers about three minutes to find the right scientist for me."

Concept giggled. "Salmon Jo wants to hatch a Cretinous Male!"

"No, Salmon Jo wants to give—to give—" Banner couldn't talk for laughing. She finally spat out the taboo phrase. "She wants to give birth to a Cretinous Male!"

"Maybe Salmon Jo should go live with the Barbarous Ones," Concept sang out. Salmon Jo rolled her eyes as Concept and Banner laughed, but she didn't seem angry. Rubric was angry for her. Well, maybe at her. Salmon Jo didn't seem to understand what a big deal today was.

"Why do you like Cretinous Males so much?" Banner teased. "Is it the hair covering their entire bodies? Or is it their spiny peanuts hanging off them?"

"Penises," Filigree Sue corrected. "Not peanuts."

"Were they really spiny?" Concept asked. "I never heard that."

"Yeah," Banner said. "Like male cats. There's a pack of feral cats in the courtyard behind Blue Dorm, and they scream every night, all summer long. Because the male cats have spiny peanuts, and it hurts the cats when they have sex. Male humans were the same."

"I'm not sure how similar human anatomy is to cat anatomy," Salmon Jo said.

Rubric thought she might throw up. This talk of Cretinous Males was not helping her nervous state. As far as she was concerned, all the girls were Hollyhocks.

Other girls were going into the auditorium. "Let's go in," Rubric said. "I want to get good seats."

"What's the rush?" Salmon Jo asked. "It's Panna Lobe. She's going to talk for half an hour about irrelevant details before she tells us who our mentors are."

"Still," Rubric said and headed for the door. The others followed. Salmon Jo grabbed Rubric's hand as they entered the room. One of the things Rubric was beginning to learn about Salmon Jo was that large groups of people made her nervous. And all the sixteen-year-olds from all the different dorms were there, about fifty girls. They only had all-class assemblies a few times a year. Banner and Concept grabbed the last two seats in the front row. Rubric and the others sat right behind them. Feeling hyperalert, Rubric found herself noticing every detail of her surroundings, like the initials someone had carved into the arm of her chair.

Panna Lobe, the head teacher, stepped up to the podium. She was a tall woman with a regal bearing who wore her hair in an old-fashioned, flower-entwined coronet braid. From her experience in the academy musical, Rubric knew that Panna Lobe was strict but had a good heart. There was total silence as Panna Lobe began speaking.

"You are embarking on one of the most special transitions in a girl's life," she said. "You are growing up, from girls into Pannas, and having a mentor is one of the most important parts of growing up. The moment when you meet your mentor for the first time will be a symbol of the entire history of Society."

Rubric didn't want to hear about the history of Society. She wanted to hear the name of her mentor.

"Cast your mind centuries back in time, to the founding of Society. At that time, the world was beset by poverty, inequality, and genetic randomness. The advent of universal cretinism in males seemed to spell doom for the human race. At the final moment, Doctors saved humanity by discovering how to create human life without the animalistic and outdated method of sexual reproduction. The Doctors chose three hundred specimens of exquisite womanhood to be the templates for all future generations to come. And thus Society was born, and in this great nation called Society we have three hundred Jeepie Types. Every Panna in Society is one of these three hundred Jeepie Types, and we are all replicated from those three hundred long-ago women. Later, scientific advances allowed the Doctors to create nonhuman Klons, subtly different from humans on a molecular level, and of course, they too are taken from the same three hundred Jeepie Types. I hope none of you ever forgets that the origin of the word Jeepie is *G P*—Genotype Phenotype."

Salmon Jo shot Rubric a look. As expected, Panna Lobe was maundering on about stuff they all knew already. Rubric was too anxious to respond.

"Up until now, none of you has ever met your Jeepie Similar—someone of your Jeepie Type. Think how carefully Society is designed, just to ensure that you will never come across a Jeepie Similar until you are ready! But now it is time.

"You have each heard so much about your Jeepie Type. Your Jeepie Type determines all your attributes: your looks, your tastes, your aptitudes, your weaknesses, and your personality. And now, at last, you will meet a mentor who is genetically identical to yourself."

She paused, and Rubric was sure she was going to read the list. But instead she went on. "A word of caution! Not every moment with your mentor will be embroidered with leaves of myrtle. Sometimes conflict arises, precisely because you and your mentor will be so similar."

Nanny Klon had talked about Salmon Jo's Jeepie Type having trouble with mentors. Maybe this was what she meant.

"And, of course, you must remember that you will not grow up to be completely identical to your mentor. There is a slight degree of originality among Jeepie Similars that is the very spice of life!"

Just read the list, Rubric silently pleaded.

As though she had heard, Panna Lobe picked up her screen. "I will now share the matches with you."

The list was not alphabetical, so Rubric was on the edge of her seat with every name. "Filigree Sue. Matched with Panna Autumn, owner of unique poodles."

It wasn't the woman Filigree Sue had been talking about, but Rubric had heard of her. Filigree Sue was clapping her hands. Rubric gave her a hug and congratulated her. She didn't recognize the names of the Pannas that Banner and Concept were matched with, but they squealed with pleasure and hugged each other. She sent them pulses with graphics of balloons, flowers, and shoes.

It seemed as though most of the girls had been covered before Panna Lobe finally read, "Rubric Anne. Matched to Panna Stencil Pavlina, artist."

Rubric grinned. She couldn't wait to meet Panna Stencil Pavlina. Her screen filled up with congratulatory pulses. But there was still a trace of fear in her stomach. She realized she was more worried about Salmon Jo's match than her own.

"Salmon Jo, matched with Panna Madrigal Sue, Hatchery scientist."

"Wait, what do you mean, *Hatchery*?" Salmon Jo blurted out, frowning.

Rubric was embarrassed. No one else had interrupted.

"Panna Madrigal is an eminent scientist at the Hatchery," Panna Lobe said. "She is closely involved with the creation of all our city's Hatchlings and coordinates with other cities' Hatcheries. She probably helped create every girl in this room."

"I have no interest in the Hatchery," Salmon Jo said shrilly. "I want to work with someone who's working on the Cretinous Male issue. I want to do research."

Behind her, Rubric heard a few snickers. She hated when she was ashamed of Salmon Jo. She didn't understand how, on the one hand, she could be madly in love with Salmon Jo and think she was perfect, and yet on the other hand she intermittently thought Salmon Jo was a total thicko.

"Panna Madrigal is very highly respected in her field," Panna Lobe said gently. "I assure you, she'll put you right to work. There are no scientists of your Jeepie Type working on the Cretinous Male issue. To be honest, I don't think anyone is working on that issue. There's no practical application."

Banner and Concept were both shaking with silent laughter and typing furiously on their screens. Rubric burned with a combination of anger, disgust, and defensiveness. She didn't know if she was more angry with those girls or with Salmon Jo.

"But my Jeepie Type tends toward pure science," Salmon Jo insisted. "I find it really hard to believe that none of my Jeepie Similars is interested in something that fascinates me. And you said the matches with our mentors were up to us! That we would have the final decision."

Concept was making a gagging sound. Rubric craned her neck to look over her shoulder and read the pulse that Banner had sent to Concept.

The screen read, *Salmon Jo wants to hatch a Cretinous Male—so she can sleep with it!*

Rubric's ears burned. This was the most depraved remark she had ever heard in her life. And it was about her own schatzie.

"I'm sure we can work something out, Salmon Jo," Panna Lobe said. "Of course, everything you do is completely your choice. No one forces you to do anything. But we have to talk later. There are girls who haven't heard their matches yet while you sit here and argue with me. That's hardly following the Golden Rule, is it?"

Salmon Jo got up and stormed out of the room. Rubric thought about following her. But in the end she decided to stay.

CHAPTER FOUR

Rubric was at her desk, drawing on her screen, when her window sash pushed up. Outside, a pale hand gripped the windowsill. She felt her heart jump, and she almost spilled a glass of water all over her screen. Salmon Jo's other hand came next, then her head, and then she was hauling herself into the dorm room.

"Can you not pulse me first when you're about to climb in my window?" Rubric asked. "You scared me to death."

"Sorry," Salmon Jo said, panting.

Rubric didn't even bother to ask why Salmon Jo thought it was necessary to shimmy up a pipe and onto the fire escape, rather than just coming to the door of Yellow Dorm and walking in like a normal person. The truth was, Salmon Jo had too much energy. She needed lots of physical exercise every day or she started to get cranky. But she didn't have enough esprit de corps to join a sports team. Every day, she ran around the campus a few times. Not the sedate jogging that other people did, in special running costumes. More as if she were being chased by a hungry bear. Salmon Jo ran fast but didn't look graceful—her arms flapped in an ungainly way. On days when it was raining hard, she liked to break into the underground maintenance tunnels and do sprints.

Rubric flopped down on her feather beanbag chair. The cloth cover of the chair had just been cleaned, and now it smelled like lavender. The Cleaning Klon in Yellow Dorm knew that lavender was Rubric's favorite scent. Salmon Jo nestled beside her, and Rubric made room for her.

Salmon Jo kissed her lips, and then kissed her ear. Her warm breath stirred on Rubric's neck. But Rubric wasn't in the mood for kisses. She was still too cross with Salmon Jo.

"Did you talk to Panna Lobe?" Rubric blurted out. "Salmon Jo, you were a total Hollyhock at that assembly."

Salmon Jo shuddered.

"I talked to her," Salmon Jo said finally. She looked down at her short-clipped fingernails as if she needed to concentrate on them.

"And?"

"I said I'd accept that mentor at the Hatchery."

"What did she say to convince you?"

Salmon Jo shrugged.

Rubric hated when Salmon Jo clammed up like this. She kicked her foot. "Tell me *something*," she insisted.

"So you know the way Hollyhock was taken away for a kidney transplant?"

"Is this relevant?"

"I don't know. I hope not. But don't you think she should have come back by now?"

"That's true," Rubric said. "It shouldn't take that long to recover. It must have been her bad kidneys that made her act so veruckt."

"I don't know about that. I used to think maybe she died during the operation, and they didn't want to tell us because we were too young to know."

"Maybe," Rubric said. "They're always trying to protect us. But maybe she just went to another academy. Did Panna Lobe talk about Hollyhock?"

"No."

Sometimes Salmon Jo could be so irritating that Rubric wanted to shake her. "Why are you asking me about her, then?"

"No reason." Salmon Jo pressed her face into the beanbag chair.

Suddenly Rubric realized Salmon Jo was scared.

"Schatzie, tell me," she whispered. "You can tell me anything." She stroked Salmon Jo's soft cheek.

Salmon Jo lifted her face from the beanbag and muttered, "I was wondering if they took Hollyhock away for treatment."

Rubric struggled to understand. "Treatment is, like, when they lock you up and give you brain medication and electric shocks and stuff. Pannas and girls—humans—don't get treatment. Only Klons who are veruckt. If something goes wrong and they go bad."

"Yeah, that's what I thought too. That's not what Panna Lobe said."

Rubric started to feel scared too. "What did she say about treatment?"

"That in certain rare instances it can happen to humans too. She said it's so shameful, they always cover up when a human has to have treatment, so people don't really know about it. Or just no one talks about it. So I started thinking about Hollyhock and all the weird stuff she said. Maybe there was nothing wrong with her kidneys. Maybe they didn't have any medication that could help her, and they had to take her away for treatment."

Salmon Jo didn't say anything for a while. Rubric wanted to prod her more, but she made herself stay quiet. If she kept badgering Salmon Jo, she would just get all belligerent.

"The good news," Salmon Jo said finally, with a crooked smile, "is that a lot of women of my Jeepie Type become Doctors. In fact, forty percent of Doctors are my Jeepie Similars."

"Wow!" Rubric said. It would be the most prestigious thing in the whole world if she had a Doctor for a schatzie. Doctors ran Society. "Some of the Doctors I see on edfotunement do look a bit like you. You know, if you had a lot of wrinkles. So what's the bad news?"

"Apparently a lot of women of my Jeepie Type have a crisis during their late teens or early twenties. Panna Lobe said they never told me this before because it might mess me up. If my Jeepie Type does well, they usually become Doctors. And some aren't chosen for careers and are just part of the happy majority. But some of the ones who don't do very well are set to work supervising the Kapo Klons. She called it being a manager."

Rubric gasped. The Kapo Klons had the job of bossing around the other Klons and making sure they were doing what they were supposed to do. That way, humans wouldn't have to waste valuable time dealing directly with Klons, and humans could get on with their business of achieving personal fulfillment. But, naturally, the Kapo Klons needed to have some humans above them to check that everything was going smoothly. There were only a few Jeepie Types that this kind of career appealed to, not enough to fill all the positions. So it was the only career that humans could be compelled to do. Any other career was purely on a voluntary basis, but the Doctors could actually tell a person they had to supervise Kapo Klons. It was almost like a punishment.

"Not only that," Salmon Jo said, nestling farther into the beanbag chair and pulling the neck of her tunic up around her chin, "Panna Lobe said some women of my Jeepie Type were so messed up they weren't even allowed to supervise the Kapo Klons. Some of them had to have treatment."

"This is all totally veruckt!" Rubric said. "I think she was just trying to scare you. I don't believe it."

But Rubric did believe it. She knew every Jeepie Type was different, but Salmon Jo seemed *more* different than anyone else. And she did all this veruckt stuff like climbing walls and breaking into tunnels. Panna Lobe had once told the class that Salmon Jo's Jeepie Type had a predilection for breaking rules. And since Society didn't have any rules beyond the Golden Rule, Salmon Jo had to invent rules to break.

"She did scare me," Salmon Jo said. "Especially since no one at academy ever tells you what to do, or that you're doing something wrong. It was like she was saying there was something wrong with me intrinsically. She said they create very few people of my Jeepie Type because of these problems."

"It doesn't make sense," Rubric said. "The Jeepie Types chosen were from the three hundred most intelligent, healthy, well-adjusted women. Why would the original Doctors have picked someone who could have problems?"

"Panna Lobe explained that in former times many creative and intelligent people did something called Thinking Outside The Box, which involved being unruly and difficult. So even though The Box no longer exists, this trait has persisted. And my Jeepie Type can make great Doctors. So that's why they keep creating my Jeepie Type."

"I guess your Jeepie Type either turns out really great or, um…"

"Exactly," Salmon Jo said. "Or down in flames. Anyway, after she told me all this, I agreed to the mentor match she proposed."

"It sounds like she knows what she's talking about," Rubric said.

Salmon Jo frowned. "I still feel kind of…I dunno, manipulated. But I don't want to end up some loser who needs treatment. Do you still like me?"

"Of course!" Rubric said. "I'll make that clear to you."

Rubric kissed her. Salmon Jo's lips were soft and warm on hers. She felt a familiar falling feeling. She could almost believe that everything was fine, or even perfect.

But then Salmon Jo broke away to say, "Panna Lobe said some women of my Jeepie Type, the ones who went bad, not only got treatment…they even got redistributed."

Rubric felt a chill. "Humans don't get redistributed," she said. "They really don't. That's ridiculous."

"She said it. Real fast."

"You must have heard her wrong. Because you were upset. Maybe she said that Klons of your Jeepie Type have been redistributed. Not Pannas."

Salmon Jo didn't answer, but she drew even closer to Rubric. She was almost crowding Rubric off the beanbag chair. Rubric didn't complain. She just stroked Salmon Jo's wiry hair.

CHAPTER FIVE

On the day they met their mentors for the first time, Salmon Jo got up at dawn. She had stayed over in Rubric's room.

"I'm going running in the city," she told Rubric, who cracked one eye open. "Finally! I am so sick of circumnavigating the campus. Do you realize I have actually run around the campus more than a thousand times? I calculated it."

Rubric had been hoping Salmon Jo would take the trolley with her later. Neither of them had ever been off campus without Klons and teachers before, and Rubric was a little nervous about getting around the city.

As it turned out, Rubric had no trouble figuring out the route by herself. It felt funny to walk through the wrought-iron gates of the campus, all by herself, without teachers or Nanny Klons, for the first time. She was planning to ask the Security Klon where to catch the Number 12 Trolley, but she saw a sign for it directly outside the entrance to campus. The hardest part was getting on the trolley, which slowed down but didn't stop. The Conductor Klon showed her where to swipe her card and explained where she needed to get off in the city center.

The city unfolded before Rubric's eyes, a mixture of the golden spires of yesteryear and the more recent spherical buildings. Rubric watched the street scene with interest: the pedestrians, the Dog Walking Klons, the bicyclists who weaved skillfully between the trolleys, the Pedicab Klons who peddled furiously to pull their passengers up the hills. She pictured Salmon Jo running wildly through these crowded streets. The trolley passed the Singing Fountain, which Rubric had visited during several annual trips. It was a beautiful day, and the sunshine made the peak of Mount Sileza sparkle in the distance. Last year her dorm had gone to Mount Sileza for its annual trip. She wondered if she and Salmon Jo could go there for a romantic hike, since Salmon Jo liked the outdoors so much. Rubric's nervousness changed to exhilaration at traveling by herself in the city for the first time.

Panna Stencil Pavlina's apartment building was just a few blocks from where Rubric got off the trolley. It was about ten stories high and looked new. Golden dogs guarded the atrium of the building. Rubric wondered if the gold in their fur made them short-lived, like some fancy breeds of dogs. She had read about people who had to change their dogs every few weeks because they didn't live longer. Some people really loved breeding dogs and found personal fulfillment in that. Rubric didn't think she would enjoy it. She would much rather be an artist, like Panna Stencil Pavlina.

Rubric rang Panna Stencil Pavlina's doorbell. A Serving Klon in a dark tunic with *Gerda* embroidered on the chest answered the door. Gerda led Rubric into the living room and took her cloak. Rubric liked the tastefully appointed living room. It was nice to be in such an opulent setting after the plain campus. Another Gerda, this one wearing a yellow tunic, came in with a tray of apples, carrots, and celery and a glass of lemonade. The lemonade had ice cubes in the shape of swans. Rubric munched the celery and apples. She didn't like carrots. She supposed that liking carrots must not be a genetic trait. Or maybe they were an acquired taste.

It was hard for her to sit still and wait. Her heart was pounding with anticipation, as if she were running a race instead of sitting on an ottoman.

A beaded curtain swished open, and Panna Stencil Pavlina strode into the room. Rubric caught her breath at how beautiful she was. Perhaps she could be that beautiful someday! Panna Stencil Pavlina was only about two inches taller, but she wore her long hair dyed black and piled on her head in coils. Her eyes were warm.

"I'm so glad to meet you, my dear," Panna Stencil Pavlina said and leaned over and kissed her on the cheek.

"It's a real honor, Panna Stencil Pavlina," Rubric said. She couldn't believe she was meeting her Jeepie Similar for the very first time.

Panna Stencil Pavlina smiled. "Drop the Panna," she said. "You can just call me Stencil Pavlina."

"Great," Rubric said.

"Did you bring your portfolio? I'd love to see it."

"Oh, I don't have a portfolio." Why didn't she have one? She should have realized that's what real artists did.

Stencil Pavlina looked disappointed, but she said, "Don't fret, my dear. We can just skip the chitchat, and I'll show you my art right away. Let's not waste any time. Come with me."

They walked through the spacious apartment. As they passed the kitchen, Rubric spied one Gerda, the one in the yellow tunic, cooking something that smelled divine. The other Gerda was plumping up pillows in the bedroom. Previously, Rubric had thought it was affected to have a set of identical Serving Klons, but now she decided to keep an open mind.

The last and largest room was Stencil Pavlina's studio. It was bright and airy, and the ceiling was covered with sculptures of birds. Some were beautiful birds and some were scary birds of prey. They were made of some brown, translucent material that must have been lightweight, since they were hanging from the ceiling. Rubric thought it might be some kind of resin. She couldn't believe the technical skill Stencil Pavlina must have to produce such detailed and realistic plumage. She had to admit she was feeling a touch of celebrity awe.

Gradually, she became aware of the other art in the room and stopped staring at the ceiling. A lot of it was incredibly creepy and sad. Anguished faces, too-realistic hearts covered with boils and scars. The most striking thing, in the center of the room, was a large sculpture of a slaughtered unicorn, its mangled limbs and entrails souping onto the floor. She wasn't sure what material the unicorn was made of.

"Wow," Rubric managed to say. Stencil Pavlina's early art—what Rubric had seen before—had been so lighthearted. What had happened to her? Whenever Rubric had pictured meeting her mentor for the first time, she had imagined they would chatter happily together and they would understand each other perfectly. She had never envisioned being intimidated and puzzled by her mentor. Or being completely tongue-tied.

"Is this all recent work?" she asked.

"I haven't really been working on anything lately. The muse has not called on me." She gestured to the slaughtered unicorn. "So what are you experiencing when you look at this piece?"

"I don't know," Rubric said. She felt thicko. "I don't know what it's about."

"Go on, take a stab," Stencil Pavlina encouraged. "There's no right or wrong. I'm just curious what you get out of it."

"Um, I guess a unicorn is a symbol of happiness and girlish innocence," Rubric hazarded. "But a unicorn is an extinct animal."

"Mythical, actually," Stencil Pavlina said. "They were never real."

"Oh." Rubric felt even more thicko.

"Please, keep going!"

"Since the unicorn has been killed, I guess that means...um, whatever it is, it's not good."

"That's wonderful," Stencil Pavlina enthused. "You've really hit the nail on the head. The dead unicorn is my metaphor for the emptiness, betrayal, and ultimate sterility of art."

"That's pretty chilling," Rubric said slowly. "For me, art is an unending fountain of happiness and inspiration. I don't see how it could cease to be the greatest delight of my life."

"Yes, I felt like that at your age too," Stencil Pavlina said. "Nurture that feeling. Keep it alive as long as you can."

Rubric felt an icy finger of doom trace across her heart.

Stencil Pavlina pulled on a bell rope that dangled from the ceiling. A Gerda appeared.

"More lemonade for our guest, Gerda," Stencil Pavlina said, stroking Gerda's arm. Her gesture gave Rubric the creeps. It seemed almost sexual. Aside from the ick factor, how could a Klon be capable of consenting to sexual stuff with a human?

Gerda bowed and left the room.

"The Gerdas are a great consolation to me," Stencil Pavlina said. "It is sad that art and literature are all our Jeepie Type has to cling to. And yet they are not enough to get us through this life."

Could this be some kind of test, Rubric wondered. Was Stencil Pavlina deliberately tormenting her?

"You may find that to be the case for yourself," Rubric said with as much dignity as she could muster. "But things will be different for me."

Panna Stencil Pavlina blinked. Gerda returned noiselessly to give Rubric her lemonade. Rubric took a big gulp. She had forgotten the big bird-shaped ice cubes, and some of the lemonade dribbled out of the sides of her mouth.

"I'm glad you have such strength of character, Rubric. I respect that," Stencil Pavlina said, with a hollow, artificial laugh.

Rubric didn't feel like she had strength of character, not with lemonade all over her chin. She wiped it with the back of her hand. Her hand was shaking. She stuffed it in her pocket, but the hand holding the glass was rattling it with her tremors.

Get a grip, Rubric told herself. *Don't be intimidated by the Panna. She's really weird, and you don't have to take her seriously.* But then Rubric was swept by a wave of disappointment more desolating than any feeling she had ever known. For if Panna Stencil Pavlina was just a big weirdo, what was the point of this?

Stencil Pavlina was saying something about the amazing work they were going to do together. Rubric concentrated on nodding and looking interested even though her mentor's words were just flowing meaninglessly by her. The birds on the ceiling caught her attention again. They were really something. At the very least, Stencil Pavlina was a master craftswoman. Rubric didn't have the first clue how to make stuff like that.

"Are the birds on the ceiling made of resin?" Rubric interrupted.

Stencil Pavlina nodded. "Good eye."

"And what material is the unicorn?"

"I sculpted it from a polylactic acid block and then spackled it."

"I'd like to learn how to do those things," Rubric said.

"Then I will teach you, my dear," Stencil Pavlina said. Could it be that she seemed a little relieved to have a specific agenda? "I would very much like to collaborate with you. I have so much to share with you, and your youthful presence will inspire me."

For the rest of the visit, Panna Stencil Pavlina was pleasant to Rubric. She confined her conversation to describing the properties of different materials. By the time Rubric left, she had learned a lot of useful information. And her hands had almost stopped shaking.

CHAPTER SIX

It had been Rubric's perfect day. She loved being on the loose in the city with Salmon Jo. They were both embarrassed to be using their maps of the city, a dead giveaway of being sixteen-year-old academy students, brand-new to leaving campus. There were a lot of other girls out today, clutching their maps. So they tried to navigate without the maps, and they didn't mind getting lost. They did all the tourist things first and ate their packed lunches by the Singing Fountain. They had seen a key-exchanging ceremony taking place on Karela Bridge, with two resplendently dressed Pannas exchanging vows of undying love. Salmon Jo had smiled and squeezed Rubric's hand, and Rubric couldn't help wondering what kind of dress she would wear if she and Salmon Jo ever exchanged keys someday. She had taken her schatzie to her new favorite place, the art-materials center. It was known as Pearl, probably because it was in an opalescent spherical building in the Uterine Celebratory style of forty years ago. Rubric loved everything about Pearl. By tradition, all the wares were laid out without rhyme or reason, so artists could browse and become inspired. If you wanted something specific, you went to the appropriate desk and a Klon would fetch it for you. Rubric couldn't really get anything with her piddling student rationing credits, but it was fun to window-shop.

Now they were at the Comfort Station downtown because they weren't ready to go back to campus yet. There were Comfort Stations sprinkled throughout the city, every few miles. They all had the same big glowing sign, a luminous tube in the shape of a piece of toast. The Comfort Station served unlimited tea and toast to all humans, and there were cots in the back if you were traveling and needed a place to sleep. It was really designed for rash, intemperate Pannas who used up all their rationing credits before the month was over and had nothing to eat. But it was open twenty-four hours, so it was a great place for young people. Even though the furnishings and the decor in the Comfort Station were sort of minimalistic, Rubric thought it had a great atmosphere. It made her feel very worldly to be out late at night at the Comfort Station with her schatzie.

The big screen in the Comfort Station was showing *Who Shall Be My Schatzie?*, the popular edfotunement show about a Panna who has to choose between sixteen women, all the same Jeepie Type. But it was obvious who she was going to pick, so Rubric and Salmon Jo had stopped watching.

"Everyone at the Hatchery has memorized all the Jeepie Types by number," Salmon Jo said. "When one Panna met me, she said, 'Oh good, another forty-two. We love forty-twos.'"

"Weird," Rubric said. "What number am I?"

"You're eight. Apparently eights and forty-twos are perfect for each other."

"I guess you really like it at the Hatchery." Rubric was trying not to sound bitter, but just a little bitterness leaked out.

Salmon Jo didn't even notice, she was considering the question so deeply. "I like some things about it. The people are all very smart, and they don't mind taking the time to teach me stuff. It's interesting but not really my kind of thing."

"What is your kind of thing?" Rubric teased.

"You," said Salmon Jo. "You are my kind of thing." She kissed Rubric on the ear. "But I wish they would let me see the proprietary data on how they engineer the Klons to be nonhuman. I need more data, to understand certain things."

"Well, I'm sure that's totally classified. What if you told the Barbarous Ones?"

Salmon Jo snorted. "The Barbarous Ones are happy living in trees and giving birth. They don't care how to make Klons."

"I can't believe that. If they had Klons, they could have such happy lives. What are the Barbarous Ones doing all day? Doing their own laundry and cooking food, like great big Klons, right?"

"They're too thicko to even want happy lives," Salmon Jo said. "And how could anyone tell them any secrets? You'd have to pass through the fence to their Land."

"Okay, fine, but the Hatchery still isn't going to give an academy student that kind of information."

"All I really want to know is who's in charge of that process. And no one seems to know. Or they're all lying."

"That's ridiculous!" Rubric said.

"I asked twenty-one of twenty-one people working in that office. They all say that's not their area, and they don't know whose it is. So whose area is it? Why all the secrecy?"

When Salmon Jo started worrying about a problem, she was a dogged little terrier until she solved it. It didn't seem to matter if the problem was big or small. She could obsess over a missing jar lid, or what to wear, or the meaning of life, or the Four Color Problem. It was all the same to her.

"And then there are other things that no one can explain to me," Salmon Jo said. "Like, why is the success rate for hatching humans one hundred percent? And the success rate for Klons is so low?"

Rubric rolled her eyes. "It's ten o'clock at night. It's too late to talk about numbers. Try me another time."

"Oh, am I boring you? We could go on an adventure."

"What kind of adventure?" Rubric asked.

❖

Forty minutes later, Rubric and Salmon Jo were breaking into the Hatchery.

"It's not breaking in," Salmon Jo insisted. "They put access on my card."

They were standing in front of the entrance, which was a rust-covered revolving metal gate in the shape of an egg slicer.

"It's possible this is a bad idea," Rubric said. She was trying not to giggle. Being anxious made her giggle, and she was trying to break that habit. She had noticed that Stencil Pavlina, for all her faults, never lost her cool. Rubric wanted to emulate that one habit.

"No rule but the Golden Rule," Salmon Jo quoted flippantly. "Right?"

"This might be breaking the Golden Rule," Rubric said.

"Absolutely not. If I had a Hatchery, I wouldn't mind if people visited in the middle of the night."

"Did they tell you that you could bring your schatzie here?"

"No," Salmon Jo said.

"Did they tell you *not* to bring your schatzie here?" Rubric asked.

Salmon Jo swiped her card in the reader. There was a click from inside the revolving gate.

"Okay, squish up to me," Salmon Jo instructed.

Rubric pressed herself against Salmon Jo's back. Salmon Jo was shorter than her, so it was like stacking a tablespoon on a teaspoon. It was a tight squeeze for Salmon Jo and Rubric to both fit inside the gate's compartment. They shuffled around until they were released on the other side. Now they were standing in a dimly lit atrium.

"As I see it, if they wanted to keep people from bringing their schatzies in, they would make it harder," Salmon Jo said.

"They just never expected anyone could be as strange as you," said Rubric.

"They should. They created me. Panna Madrigal told me the original of our Jeepie Type was something called a hacker, and that's why I am the way I am."

"What is that?" Rubric asked. "Some kind of butcher? A killer? Some other social deviant?"

"I don't know," Salmon Jo admitted. "I was afraid to ask."

They walked into the hallway, and Salmon Jo flipped on the light. The floor was industrial-grade rubber linoleum. The walls had grubby white paint up to eye level, and then a pretty robin's egg blue going up the rest of the wall. Salmon Jo gestured to different doors as they passed them.

"This is the lab where they insert the Jeepie Type nuclei into the enucleated ova and apply a shock to make the cell divide. That's the most fun part, obviously. I only got to tour that lab once. They said after I've been here a few months, I can help out in there. My card doesn't open that door so I can't show you. The zygote freezer is over there. Wow, do they get mad if you leave the door open by mistake!"

Salmon Jo pulled open the heavy metal door, and a cloud of cold air roiled out. Rubric shivered and peered inside. Disappointingly, it looked like any walk-in freezer. Its wire shelves were lined with metal canisters labeled with arcane numbers. There was also a tub of ice cream.

"Panna Madrigal has a sweet tooth, just like me," Salmon Jo said. She closed the freezer door and checked it twice to make sure it was really shut. They passed another revolving metal gate. "That leads to the nurseries. As soon as they decant the Hatchlings and examine them, they whisk them right in there where Klons start taking care of them. Now, that room is where Doctors examine the Hatchlings. It's boring, just a bunch of tables and scales and cabinets. I saw a Doctor in there once, though! This chute in the wall leads to the high-heat compost unit. The defective Hatchlings they have to put down are disposed of there. Okay, this room is totally cool! You're going to love the fetus room!"

Salmon Jo swiped her card and they entered the fetus room.

CHAPTER SEVEN

The fetus room was like a different world. The lighting was soft, unlike the harsh, flickering overhead in the hallway. Gentle music was playing. The temperature was toasty. Abstract art in bold primary colors hung on the walls. A profusion of plants filled the room, so that at first Rubric hardly noticed the bubbling gestation tanks.

"Oh!" she cried, and ran up to one of them. Inside the spherical tank, in a fizzy blue fluid, was a fetus. Its head seemed too big for its body. It was all curled up, and its little eyes were squeezed shut, but its tiny fists shot out. Every now and then the tank rotated slightly, and the fetus adjusted position.

"That one is seven months," Salmon Jo said. "Aren't they amazing? I can't decide if they're more creepy or more cute."

"I've seen pictures, but it's so different to see one in person," Rubric said, awed. Tears welled up in her eyes, and she blinked them away. Salmon Jo took her hand.

"Is it human or Klon?" Rubric asked.

"I don't know," Salmon Jo said. "The tanks aren't marked, and no one will explain it to me. Maybe the Klon process happens later, and at this point they're all on track to be human?"

The little fetus kicked. Then its hand opened and closed.

"It's waving!" Rubric said. "It's waving at me!"

"Talk to it," Salmon Jo said.

"What?"

"Talk to it," Salmon Jo said. "The scientists say it's good for the fetuses if we talk to them. That's one of my jobs. I have to talk to them for an hour every day. To a different one every day, so I don't develop a false rapport which could be unhealthy."

"You never told me that! That's the most interesting thing I've heard about your job. Okay, here goes. Hello, fetus!" She felt shy. "You're doing a great job growing. I bet you'll become a magnificent girl! Um, I don't know what else to say."

"Yeah, I have that problem too," Salmon Jo said. "I read to them a lot. Sometimes I sing."

Rubric giggled. Salmon Jo had a terrible singing voice. "You're probably warping their development."

"These ones will be decanted in just a couple of months. That should be exciting. Come look at some of the others," Salmon Jo said.

Some of the fetuses were just froglike blobs. Salmon Jo said they were called embryos. A few of the tanks looked empty, but Salmon Jo insisted they contained something really small called blastocysts. Rubric was surprised to see a glossy black cat curled up under one of the tanks, sleeping.

"They say being around pets is good for the fetuses," Salmon Jo said. "I can't see how, but there's a lot of data supporting the claim. And the cats like to lie under the tanks because they're so warm."

"I'm surprised they don't need someone monitoring the tanks at night," Rubric said. "What if something happened?"

"Actually, someone comes in every three hours," Salmon Jo said. She checked the watch hanging around her neck. "So maybe we should move along."

Rubric put her hand on the nearest tank, which held a jellyfish-like glob with a barely recognizable head and dots for eyes. "Good-bye, little thing," she cooed. It was amazing to get to see the fetuses, to watch the miracle of life in action. She thought this should be part of academy students' annual trip.

They closed the door of the fetus room behind them. "One more stop," Salmon Jo said. "The office. It's pretty boring, but it's where I spend most of my time." They went through the last door in the hallway. As Salmon Jo had warned, it was just a large room with hexagonal areas enclosed by bamboo screens to give people private space. Every desk and table was cluttered with terminals, handheld screens, and other equipment. The walls were covered with graphics. A lot of the chairs seemed to be held together with electrical tape. In short, the office was a mess.

"So what is it that people do here?"

"Planning. They crunch a lot of numbers to see how many Klons and humans they need to hatch to keep the city's population steady, and what Jeepie Types. And how many blastocysts they should create to get that number, since a lot of Klon fetuses lose viability in the tanks. And a lot of the Klons are hatched defective and have to be put down."

For the first time, Rubric became interested in Salmon Jo's boring numbers problem. "Really? It's just the Klons that are hatched defective?"

"Yeah. No one told me, I figured that out myself from running the numbers. Literally all the humans are perfect. And all the defective ones that are put down and composted are Klons. Only around forty percent of Klons are healthy, nondefective Hatchlings that are brought to the nursery. It seems like someone should be working on that problem. There must be some kind of design flaw."

"Hmm, when do the fetuses become Klons?" Rubric mused. "Is it when they stick the nucleus into the ovum or whatever you said? The thing they do in the lab?"

"No. They use the same genetic material for both Klons and humans. They told me that much."

"Maybe they know which ones are going to be Klons, but they're keeping it a secret." Rubric felt like there was something obvious that was eluding her, but she couldn't put her finger on it.

"What would be the point of that?" Salmon Jo said.

"Oh!" Suddenly it was all illuminated for Rubric. "It's very simple, you see! They're just not designated Klon or human until after they fail or succeed. That would explain everything. Perfect Hatchlings, automatically human. Everything that goes wrong, automatically Klon. Any perfect Hatchlings that they don't need for humans, they can become Klons too."

Salmon Jo just laughed. "That's thicko, Rubric. By the time they're hatched, the alteration, whatever it may be, has been done. They have to be decanted either as humans or Klons."

Rubric didn't like being laughed at. She stubbornly stuck by her idea. "Maybe the alteration is done after they're decanted from the tanks. Since you can't figure out when or what happens, that makes sense. They just inject some of the Hatchlings with something, and presto, they turn into Klons."

Salmon Jo looked troubled. "No process like that could exist. By the time the Hatchling humans are decanted, they are as developed as a human newborn can be and are therefore human. Even if there was a way to reverse development and stunt a human into a Klon, that would be totally unethical. Anyway, Klons are specially engineered to have certain strengths, like the ability to work harder than a human, and weaknesses, like not being as intelligent or emotionally evolved as humans. You can't do all that with a shot. It has to be done while they're fetuses in tanks."

Rubric threw up her hands. "You just showed me how the fetuses in the tanks are all the same, and now you're saying they can't be the same. And you're supposed to be the logical one! You're as thicko as a Klon."

Salmon Jo licked her lips. "Your theory, veruckt as it seems to be, is the only one that fits the facts." She went into the biggest hexagonal area. After a moment, Rubric followed her. Salmon Jo was rooting through a desk, pulling out handheld screens.

"Is this your desk?" Rubric asked. It seemed too big and with too much equipment for just an academy student being mentored.

"No, it's Panna Tensility's. As far as I can tell, she's the smartest one here and knows the most about everything."

Now Rubric was truly shocked. Salmon Jo ought not to go through other people's property. "The Golden Rule—" she said helplessly.

"The cause of science is a higher rule," Salmon Jo muttered. She was looking at a handheld screen, paging through its documents.

Higher rule, rubbish, Rubric thought. Salmon Jo was just a snoop.

"No, I can't understand it," Salmon Jo said. Her voice cracked in the middle of the sentence. "This doesn't make sense."

"Let me see," Rubric said. Salmon Jo showed it to her. But the screen only showed a spreadsheet that was a meaningless jumble to her. How could a spreadsheet make anyone so upset?

"This shows when the fetuses are designated Klon or human," Salmon Jo said. "According to this, it's not any time when they're in the tank. The Doctors designate the freshly decanted Hatchlings to be human or Klon when they examine them, in their first minutes of life."

"So what's the secret process that makes some of them Klon?" Rubric asked. She didn't have a good feeling about this.

Salmon Jo clicked through other documents for a long time. Finally, she said, "It seems to be that the Doctors put either a blue tag or white tag on the Hatchling's toe. If they get a white tag, they're human. Blue tags are for Klons."

Her words felt like a slap. Rubric gasped.

"So there's no difference between humans and Klons?" Rubric asked. She had a curious feeling, as if she were floating just above her own skin.

"Except for the tag," Salmon Jo said.

Rubric stared into Salmon Jo's amber eyes. Salmon Jo looked as troubled as Rubric felt.

"There must be another explanation," Salmon Jo said. "Something we're not thinking of."

But she couldn't come up with one.

After a while, Rubric said, "We better get back to the dorms. I don't want to get caught in here."

On the way back to the dorm, Rubric had a funny feeling. She didn't even know how to name it. It was something akin to unease. Disquiet. Rubric felt as if all her trustfulness had been washed away. Their nighttime adventure now seemed much worse than just sneaking into the Hatchery.

CHAPTER EIGHT

Rubric stayed over in Salmon Jo's room in Maroon Dorm. Rubric thought she would never fall asleep. But she must have, at some point, because she woke up to Salmon Jo shaking her.

"I'm going to the refectory," Salmon Jo was telling her. "Do you want me to bring you something to eat?"

"Some fruit," Rubric said thickly, still half asleep.

"I've been awake for hours, thinking. I'm sure now that Klons and humans are the same. It's the only thing that makes sense."

This woke Rubric up like a bucket of cold water being dumped on her head.

"But they're not like us! They're thicko and less self-aware and don't have complex emotions. We can see their primitive—" Rubric faltered and fell silent. She couldn't think of any actual examples to support her case.

"I think we just see them as less than human because we're told to see that," Salmon Jo said. "Maybe they are not as smart because they don't grow up the same way as us. Or maybe they are as smart. What is smart, anyway?"

"We can't jump to conclusions," Rubric protested. "We could have misinterpreted the whole thing. Maybe there's one piece of evidence we don't know about that explains everything."

"What does it mean to be human anyway? I'm not sure anymore what a human is," Salmon Jo said. Her thin, muscular body was vibrating with tension like the string of a musical instrument.

"I do," Rubric said crossly. "I'm a human, and so are you. You're just making it too complicated."

"I don't know," Salmon Jo said. "I don't know." She repeated herself three or four more times as she fastened her running shoes. "I'll get you some fruit. I just don't know."

Rubric was left alone with her thoughts. Suddenly she couldn't stand lying in bed anymore. She got up and dressed in yesterday's clothes. She tried to think of everything she knew about why Klons were Klons and how they got that way. It seemed she didn't know anything, no more than she knew why the sky was blue.

She took her handheld screen out of her cloak pocket and sat down at Salmon Jo's desk. She looked up *Klons hatched* and *origins of Klons* and *how Klons not humans*. All the results were simple texts for children, with lots of graphics but little content. The information was scanty and repetitive. Over and over, she read:

Klons are engineered to be different.

Klons are so different from humans.

Klons are engineered to complement us.

Nothing explained how they were different or how they were engineered. Finally, she found a more advanced text, one she remembered reading a few years ago for academy. It had no graphics and was a history of Society. She read:

During the Gendered Period of human history, male humans conspired together to subjugate the females and institute a system known as *patriarchy*, where males were in control. Because of their hormonal and neurological differences, males were typically brutal, non-nurturing, and emotionally underdeveloped, and had poor social skills. These hormonal differences also caused males to wage war, a violent conflict between societies that led to countless deaths and injuries, and poor quality of life.

Women were forced to imitate animals in order to reproduce. Like other mammals, when a male and a Panna shared a sexual experience, the Panna might become *pregnant*, meaning she would grow a fetus inside her own body, inside the uterus organ (now vestigial in women of Society). Humans were unable to control the timing of these *pregnancies*. The only way to further the human race was to share sexual experiences with men, so no matter how distasteful this was, the majority of women continued to do so. The females excreted their Hatchlings, which they called *babies* or *infants*, through a painful and dangerous process known as *childbirth*. Many women suffered serious injuries or even death during *childbirth*. In addition, in most cases women were forced to be the sole caregivers for their own young, leading to exhaustion, depression, and an unhealthy bond between *mother* and child.

The advent of Cretinous Males took the world by surprise. In 2043, the world first took note of the afflictions visited on male children, although the problem may have manifested prior to that. There is still no satisfactory explanation for the advent of the Cretinous Males, although leading theories of the day focused on the possible effects of environmental toxins on DNA. It seems the Cretinous Males suffered from a mitochondrial disorder, causing every cell in their body to have trouble producing energy, leading to both mental and physical problems. The last specimen of a non-Cretinous Male, Chien-Yeh Hwang, died in 2149, living out his final years in a combination folk museum and laboratory habitat.

The loss of male humans has only led to evolutionary improvement. In the twenty-second century, Doctors perfected the form of SCNT (Somatic Cell Nuclear Transfer) that is still used today, thus ensuring the survival of our species. And so Society was created. Panna Charity Navrilova was the lead scientist on this breakthrough, and she has been immortalized by having her DNA included in our three hundred Jeepie Types. All humans alive today are genetic copies of extraordinarily healthy, notable, and well-adjusted women. Three hundred women were chosen to be the Jeepie Types that all humans in Society are replicated from. Each Jeepie Type is intelligent, thoughtful, kind, creative, and beautiful in its own way. We can all be proud of who we are. We have made war and conflict things of the past. In Society, we use discussion to solve problems and look to our Doctors for leadership.

In 2270, eminent biologist Panna Ash Franziska invented the groundbreaking genetic manipulation that creates Klons. Until that time, humans in Society were forced to degrade themselves by doing manual labor. In those distant days, not only did humans toil in lowly jobs that did not spark personal growth, such as food preparation, transportation, child care, and manual labor, but humans were also expected to clean their own clothes and dwellings. As a result, they were unable to reach their full human potential, and only a few selected humans were able to fulfill themselves with music, writing, acting, visual art, and the other lively arts. Furthermore, as oil reserves declined, it became impossible to use the labor-saving, energy-intensive devices which were prevalent at that time, such as automobiles, dishwashers, and washing machines.

Women of Society were spending more and more time carrying out meaningless activities of daily life.

Klons are truly a new species of mammal. They are created in the Hatchery alongside human Hatchlings. They are specially engineered to have superior strength and endurance to humans, but at the same time they lack the intelligence, emotional development, and sense of self that are the hallmark of being human. Although Klons are taken from the same 300 Jeepie Types as we humans, scientists have used molecular technology to alter their fundamental essence. Klons' frontal cortices are not as developed as those of humans, and thus advanced concepts remain beyond them. Their psychological makeups are also not as robust as that of humans, and so they must sometimes be given treatment. Although there are many hilarious edfotunement series about Klons being mistaken for humans, in reality, this could never occur. All Klons have identifying chips embedded in their abdomens. Klons are the perfect complement to humans, and we believe our two species will be forever entwined in an unending chain of myrtle.

In Society, we practice thelytoky and are no longer subjected to pregnancies, childbirth, and their attendant dangers. All our Hatchlings are decanted in a safe, clean Hatchery. In Society, our children are raised in dormitories by Klons who have been given the highest training.

Sadly, in the neighboring Land of the Barbarous Ones, it was fringe lunatics who were replicated rather than the cream of humanity. The benighted women there continue to engage in the outdated practices of pregnancy and childbirth. They have chosen to implant human embryos into their uterus organs, forgoing all the benefits derived from gestation in a tank. The Barbarous

Ones form unhealthy attachments to their young, smothering them with individual attention and not allowing them to enjoy dormitory life. The Barbarous Ones have no Klons and are thus doomed to a primitive life of incessant exertion. Their most repulsive practice is that they also create Cretinous Male embryos and implant them into their uterus organs, so that their land is peopled by drooling, hairy Cretinous Males. Because of Society's commitment to peace and the Golden Rule, we ignore our savage neighbors. The Fence between Society and the Land of the Barbarous Ones ensures our continuing tranquility and freedom from care.

There was more, but Rubric clicked off the screen. The last time she had read this text, she had been a bit overwhelmed by the information density. Now, she found it completely lacking. It didn't really explain anything about the Klons.

The door opened and Salmon Jo came in, clutching a huge tray of apples. Her expression now was calm and clear. Rubric could see that the uncertainty had left Salmon Jo.

"It would take me a month to eat all those apples!"

"We might need them," Salmon Jo replied obscurely.

"Let's go talk to Panna Lobe," Rubric said. "That's what you're supposed to do when you have problems, right?"

"Okay," Salmon Jo said. "But we can't tell her we were at the Hatchery last night, or that I looked at Panna Tensility's handheld screen. I don't want to get in trouble."

"Of course not," Rubric said. "Am I a thicko?"

Walking across the green, pretty campus, Rubric felt like she was in a dream. A Klon was loading a reel mower onto the back of an electric cart, and the sweet fragrance of freshly clipped grass hung in the air. There was a Klon pushing a cart full of laundry. Rubric stared at the woman, trying to see if she looked human or not. Her posture seemed different from the students and teachers surrounding her. Was that how you could tell if someone was human? One moment, Rubric would think, *That Klon just looks totally different, I can't define it, but there's just something about her that makes her not a real person.* The next moment, that difference would vanish, and Rubric felt like she was staring at a Panna who was unaccountably pushing a laundry cart. She didn't know anymore what was all in her head and what was real.

Panna Lobe greeted them warmly and asked her Klon to serve them tea. It felt reassuring to sit in her dowdy office with the dark wood paneling. The Panna sat in a plush overstuffed chair that smelled faintly of cedar and listened seriously to all they had to say. Their story didn't make a lot of sense with all the key elements left out. In the end, she just shook her head.

"Girls, what you're saying is not possible. It's inconceivable that the Doctors would perpetrate such an outrageous fraud on Society. Salmon Jo, you're bright, but that doesn't mean you can understand everything that goes on at the Hatchery. The scientists are not required to reveal all their secrets to you. You must know that Klons are specially engineered to have superior strength and endurance, but they lack our intelligence and emotional development. Rubric, you need to harness your powerful imagination to create something good, not a veruckt story like this. Only the combination of the two of you could come up with something like this! Come back and see me again next week."

They left dispirited.

"I wanted to believe her," Rubric said. "She talked, but she didn't say anything. She said the same thing I read in a text, almost word for word. You're right about this, Salmon Jo. I think you know better. I can't explain it, but I just know you're right. I feel it in my bones."

"I trust your bones," Salmon Jo said and put her arm around Rubric. Rubric drew comfort from the weight of Salmon Jo's arm.

Chapter Nine

Just because the fabric of Rubric's universe had been ripped apart was no reason for her to quit her regular routine. In fact, that was all she had to cling to. The world that she had believed in didn't exist, so what was she supposed to do with herself all day? Go to Stencil Pavlina's as she usually did.

Stencil Pavlina wanted to teach her to make a plaster cast of a clay object. "I learned this from my mentor, and now I want to teach it to you," Stencil Pavlina said, her voice throbbing with emotion. "This will be the first step in our collaboration. You see how this mentorship is an undying myrtle chain, passed down through all the generations, keeping art alive."

Rubric really didn't care about the undying myrtle chain. She was just happy to have something to keep her hands busy. Yesterday she had made a simple clay swan. The next step was making an emollient out of beeswax and olive oil. "Of course, your Klons will make this for you, but you have to be able to teach them how," Stencil Pavlina instructed. Rubric imagined this process was like cooking because it involved shredding, heating, and mixing. When it was ready, they slathered the emollient onto the clay swan. Rubric wondered how Stencil Pavlina would be able to make the final product grisly and depressing. Stencil Pavlina instructed Rubric to divide the mold with little walls, so they could cast one half at a time.

The best part so far was mixing the plaster. You had to sift calcium sulfate, a white powder, into a bucket of water. Then stir it up until it was a milkshake-like consistency. Rubric liked mixing the squishy plaster. It felt good in her hands. She had never done any activity like this before. Again, Stencil Pavlina reminded her that Klons would do this work for her, but she had to know how to teach them.

"You won't have more than one Klon at first when you move out of the dorm," Stencil Pavlina continued, warming to her subject. "If you think about it, the plaster objects you make are sort of like the Klons themselves. They're terribly similar to the clay original. But they don't have the same level of detail."

Rubric had noticed people saying weird stuff like this all the time lately. It made her wonder if everyone unconsciously knew the truth, and they had to keep saying things to perpetuate their self-deception.

She was trying so hard to suppress this thought that she accidentally blurted out another one. "Wow, if the original clay objects are so much better, why don't you make a series of clay objects instead of making all this plaster stuff?"

It came out sounding awfully snarky.

Without missing a beat, Stencil Pavlina said, "Gerda, slap her."

The Gerda who was closer to Rubric—there was no confusion about who was meant to do it—reached out and slapped Rubric's face. It stung, and it felt as though a hand was still on her cheek, even after Gerda returned to her bucket of plaster. Tiny clumps of plaster were stuck to Rubric's cheek. It confused Rubric how quickly they had ganged up on her, without stopping the flow of work. Gerda was pouring, pouring expressionlessly.

Rubric whirled to Stencil Pavlina. "Why did you do that?"

"Don't ask me why I'm not making something," Stencil Pavlina said. "I won't abide it."

"You don't slap people!" She couldn't believe she had to explain this to a Panna.

"Look, Rubric, I know when you're a teenager there's only the Golden Rule," Stencil Pavlina said. "But in the real world, you have to treat people a certain way, or they'll punish you. So you can't act like a thicko young snot nose all the time. Once you leave the dorm, you're part of Society, and you have to know your place."

Her place? "I'll show you my place," Rubric said and slapped Stencil Pavlina back. Apparently she did it pretty hard because Stencil Pavlina's head snapped back, and there was a wet plaster handprint on her face.

Stencil Pavlina's eyes flashed. "You can't slap *me*," she told Rubric. "You are supposed to slap my Klon!"

"Weird, weird, weird," Rubric declared. "You know what? You are veruckt."

"Gerda, throw a tantrum," Panna Stencil Pavlina ordered.

The other Gerda, the one who hadn't slapped Rubric, threw down the cloth she was using to rub emollient on the bird. "*Waah!*" she cried and stamped her feet. She balled her hands into fists and shook them at Rubric. "*Waah!*"

Rubric was startled at how genuine the Klon's dictated emotions seemed to be. The other Gerda just watched, slowly stirring the plaster so it wouldn't thicken and harden. Was the stirring Gerda smiling ever so slightly? Rubric's eyes darted back and forth from stirring Gerda to tantruming Gerda. Finally, she returned her gaze to Stencil Pavlina. She had often seen humans ask Klons to act out their emotions for them on edfotunement. She had believed it was in poor taste, but it had never before struck her as insane.

"I'm not impressed at all," she said.

To her surprise, Stencil Pavlina smiled a little crooked smile. "No?" she said. "Neither would I have been at your age. Gerda, that's enough."

Gerda stopped screaming and stamping.

"Why don't you take the rest of the day off?" Stencil Pavlina said. "We'll make a fresh start tomorrow. We must not stain our artistic bond with this unpleasantness."

Rubric nodded. Being around Pannas who didn't know the truth was stressing her out. She would go spend some time with someone who always made her feel better. She would visit her Nanny Klon.

CHAPTER TEN

Rubric knocked on the wall beside the doorway to Nanny Klon's room. She was trying hard to treat Klons like the humans they were. Humans had doors to their rooms, and you wouldn't go in without knocking.

"My pet!" Nanny Klon said. Her wide face crinkled into a smile.

"Can I come in, Bloom?" Rubric asked.

Nanny Klon seemed surprised at being called by her name. "Of course," she said. "What's wrong?"

"Nothing's wrong," said Rubric. Lies, lies. "Only I was going to bring you some peppermint oil and I forgot." She felt guilty. That's all she felt these days.

"Oh, what a sweet thought," said Nanny Klon. "What's that expression? I walked a thousand klicks and presented a feather as a gift."

"I've often heard that expression, but it makes no sense," Rubric said.

"I can explain that to you," Nanny Klon said. "When I was training to be a Nanny Klon, I learned hundreds of folktales from human history. You don't know until you're assigned, you see, what age child you'll be working for. So I might have been with little girls only five years old, and in that case I would need to tell them lots of stories. As it is, I need to know a lot about how to help resolve disputes and counsel people on the affairs of the heart."

"Would you tell me the story, Bloom?" Rubric asked, sitting down with Nanny Klon on the bed. "My Nanny Klon when I was small used to tell me stories."

"Certainly," said Nanny Klon. She began to tell her story, smoothing back the hair from Rubric's forehead. "Once, long ago, there was a young Panna who wanted to pay her respects to the supreme Doctor of her Society. So she got two beautiful swans and put them in two wicker baskets and began a journey of one thousand klicks. On the way, the swans got all dusty and rumpled from being locked up in those wicker baskets so long. Since the young Panna had almost reached the castle where the Doctor lived, she wished to make them more clean and presentable. Just before she arrived at the palace, she came to a lovely lake with reflecting waters. She decided to wash the swans in the lake. But those ungrateful swans! Do you know what they did?"

"They flew off," Rubric said. "Obviously. That's what I would do too. I think the Panna was a bit of a thicko not to foresee that."

"Girls of your Jeepie Type are always so judgmental," Nanny Klon said fondly. "You're right, though. The swans flew off. And the poor young Panna was left with nothing but a handful of white feathers."

"And a couple of baskets," Rubric said. "Were the two swans really girls who were under a spell of enchantment? And now they were free?"

"No, you're thinking of a different story," Nanny Klon said. "These were just swans. And the story is not about them, it's about the young Panna. So the young Panna, truly dispirited, continued the last leg of her journey to see the supreme Doctor. And when she got there, there was a whole line of people presenting gifts to the Doctor. Each more fabulous than the one before. Rubies, emeralds, diamonds, gold, that sort of thing. And when the young Panna came face-to-face with the Doctor, she presented one white feather and told her, 'I traveled one thousand klicks to bring you swans, but they flew away, and now all I have left to give you is this feather.'"

"She should have given her the baskets," Rubric said. "You can never have too many baskets."

"The Doctor was very impressed by the young Panna's sincerity," Nanny Klon continued. "So the Doctor declared that the white feather was the best gift she had ever received."

"That's thicko," said Rubric. "The Doctor was lying."

"The moral of the story, and the meaning of the expression," Nanny Klon finished doggedly, "is your intentions count for more than the value of the gift you bring. That's why I'm pleased you had the intention of bringing me peppermint oil."

"But wouldn't you prefer to have the intentions *and* the peppermint oil?" asked Rubric. "I mean, you can't bring a gift without having intended to bring it."

"But you could give a gift with an empty heart," Nanny Klon said. "Now, Rubric. Tell me what the matter is. I know you. You aren't so argumentative except when you're worried about something."

And then Rubric couldn't hold it in anymore. She spilled the whole story to Nanny Klon.

❖

"So you're not really a Klon," Rubric concluded. "Or maybe I'm a Klon too. What I mean is, there are no Klons! Only human beings! And you should be free, free to do whatever you want, like I am."

Nanny Klon's lips began to tremble. She looked very pale. "Stuff and nonsense!" she told Rubric. Her voice was quavering. "And what do you mean, free to do whatever you want? Don't you think I like what I do? Don't you think I take pride in my work, molding you young children into pillars of society? I'll have you know I'm one of the best! Without Nanny Klons like me, Society would crumble into the ground, and that's no lie! Why, you humans are too flighty and spoiled to raise your own young."

"But, Bloom—"

"Stop calling me that!" snapped Nanny Klon. And then covered her mouth.

Rubric remembered that she had only found out what Nanny Klon's name was by snooping in her private possessions.

"I'm sorry, Nanny Klon," she said.

"All right, enough of you," said Nanny Klon. She emitted a big fakey laugh, but her eyes were not laughing. "You've had your little joke, now get out of my room."

Rubric got up. Nanny Klon practically pushed her out of the room, laughing inanely as she did so.

Rubric went straight to Salmon Jo in Maroon Dorm and told her everything. While she talked, she played with the packages of oatmeal that Salmon Jo had started hoarding in her room.

"Do you ever wonder if maybe the hatching process has done something to our brains?" Rubric asked. "Like maybe we're all devolving. I can't believe that we as a Society could do something so evil. I mean, you hear about humans in the olden days, when there were males. They had wars and people dying of diseases and deformed people and poverty and global warming and people dying in childbirth and stuff like that. We look so great by comparison. But we're really not. Maybe none of us is really human anymore."

"I think this is totally a regular human thing," Salmon Jo said, smoothing Rubric's tunic down onto her back. "I've been doing a little research, and apparently slavery is almost a constant throughout human history. I was even thinking that maybe it's okay that the Klons are enslaved. I mean, we've been wrong about everything we ever thought. Maybe we're wrong about this too. It seems all the slave-owning societies had some kind of rationale, some kind of justification of why it's right. Maybe that's just the way it has to be."

"It's wrong," Rubric said. She grabbed Salmon Jo's hand and pressed it between hers. "I just know it is."

"How can we be sure of anything anymore? What is the meaning of anything we think or feel? You know we two are now the most fringe people in Society. Like, there are those vegetarian women who refuse to get organ transplants. Everyone thinks they're thickos. And we are believing something way more veruckt than them."

"Think about your Jeepie Similars," Rubric said, stroking Salmon Jo's slender fingers. She really wanted Salmon Jo to understand her. "Imagine a girl who is exactly like you. She has the exact identical DNA to you, only she was brought up to be a Klon instead of a human. She has to do menial labor, and maybe give away her cornea or anything else someone might need. How can you sleep when you know she's a human being? I keep thinking about my Jeepie Similars who are Klons. They're not creating art. They're not writing poems. They're not lying on lavender-scented pillows. It's just a complete accident that I'm me and they're them. And they're *exactly* like me. So I know how they feel about it. I know how I would feel about being a Klon. Bad!"

"Well," Salmon Jo said. "Well. They don't feel exactly the same as you would feel about it. I mean, they've been in this role since hatching. They're used to it."

Before Rubric could even argue with her, Salmon Jo burst into tears. Rubric folded her into her arms, but she didn't know what to say.

Chapter Eleven

The next day, Rubric played hooky from Stencil Pavlina's. What difference did it make if she went or not? Instead, she went to the apothecary and picked out a bottle of peppermint oil. It was her first purchase off campus, and she liked the atmosphere in the apothecary shop. The shelves were lined with glass bottles, and serious-looking Klons in white tunics waited on the Pannas and pounded mysterious substances into boluses for them. The Klon made her promise to bring the glass bottle back for reuse when the peppermint oil was gone. Rubric was looking forward to doing something nice for Nanny Klon.

But when she gave it to Nanny Klon, she just stared at her blankly.

"You know, the peppermint oil to help you drink your vial of fat every day? Like we were talking about yesterday."

Nanny Klon grabbed her arm and said, "Oh, Rubric! That is so thoughtful. Thank you!"

Rubric thought she knew why Nanny Klon was acting so oddly. "Listen, what I was telling you yesterday, forget about it. I didn't mean to upset you."

"I think I should tell you something," Nanny Klon said. "You and I have a particularly close relationship. Am I right?"

"I think so," Rubric said softly.

"Well, it's not necessary for me to tell everyone this, but I'm not the same Nanny Klon. She was reassigned last night, and I'm her replacement."

Rubric looked closely at Nanny Klon. She had the same round face, the same haircut. Was she perhaps a little bit younger? She didn't seem to have Bloom's wrinkles around her eyes. And maybe she might be a little bit thinner too. Rubric wasn't really sure.

"I tell you, I stayed up all night learning all the names and information about the students in Yellow Dorm. What a challenge! But I know how kind and considerate you are, Rubric, and that you like to be surprised with a nice cup of hot chocolate when you're up late doing your art projects. Right?"

"Yes," Rubric said faintly. "But what happened to Bloom? Why was she reassigned? Where did she go?"

Nanny Klon blinked in surprise. "My, you and I are very close!" she said. "I'm not sure, honey. They don't give me that kind of information."

"Is it something that she requested?" Rubric said. "Maybe something so that she could be closer to a friend? Or a schatzie? Maybe a Klon named Shine?" Of course, Klons weren't supposed to have schatzies, they just had snuggle buddies, since they weren't supposed to be capable of deep relationships. She desperately tried to focus on this thought, so she couldn't start to think of any bad reason why Bloom might have been reassigned. Like that Rubric might have caused trouble for her. Scheiss. She had thought of it anyway.

"It doesn't generally work that way, dear," Nanny Klon said. It was so disconcerting, the way she looked exactly like the old Nanny Klon. "Listen, dear, is it distressing to you to find that I'm a different Klon than my predecessor? I know that can be disturbing sometimes for you when you grow close to us. But you should know that I am her Jeepie Similar, I've received exactly the same training, and I've received exhaustive information about you and your likes and dislikes. I might be a bit off today—it's only my first day, I'm sure I'll know you better by tomorrow. I know there are conversations we've had that I don't remember, but you can always bring me up to speed on whatever we talked about."

"I never had a conversation with you," Rubric said flatly.

"In a way. We're interchangeable, you know."

"How many Nanny Klons have there been since I arrived at the dorm?" Rubric asked. What if there had been several and she'd never even noticed?

Nanny Klon furrowed her brow. "I don't know, dear. We usually stay somewhere for a long time."

"Then why did she leave?"

"You really are upset! I can try to find out some of these things for you, but I am not sure if you should really be interested in them. Honey, I'm sure you'll feel better about this by tomorrow. But if you really feel upset, you should definitely talk to another human about this, maybe Panna Lobe or Panna Stencil Pavlina. Or"—Rubric could see her racking her brains—"your schatzie… Tuna Jo?"

"Salmon Jo," she said.

"Yes! Tomorrow I'll remember that. You two are so close, so much in love. Maybe you should talk to her."

"I think I will. Thank you, Nanny Klon," she said politely.

"Thanks for the peppermint oil," Nanny Klon said. "I'm sure it will make my fat slide down smoothly." She squeezed Rubric's arm, and Rubric walked away.

Rubric couldn't stop a few tears from trickling down her cheek. She would never see Bloom again. And she had no one to blame but herself.

Her vision was so blurry that in the hallway she bumped into Filigree Sue.

"Rubric, what's wrong?" Filigree Sue asked.

"It's no big deal, Fil." Rubric sniffed. She didn't even know if she should tell her. But why should she have to keep it a secret? "It's just that Nanny Klon has been replaced by another Nanny Klon."

"Huh, no kidding. So?"

"So I miss her."

Filigree Sue laughed and clouted Rubric on the back of her head. "You thicko, next you'll be missing the pierogi you ate for lunch! You need to get more sleep and stop drawing pictures. I remember when you were a little child and you used to have tea parties with your dolls and gave them all different personalities. You haven't changed at all. Too much imagination is your problem. You're just another Hollyhock!"

Completely unexpectedly, Salmon Jo appeared at her side. Salmon Jo was looking particularly disheveled. Her curly hair was sticking up, and her chest was heaving as though she had been running for klicks. Rubric wondered why she wasn't at the Hatchery like she was supposed to be.

"Ru!" she gasped. "We have to leave right now. We're in mortal danger!"

"What do you mean?"

"Remember what happened to Hollyhock?" She grabbed Rubric's hand and started pulling her down the hallway.

CHAPTER TWELVE

Filigree Sue shouted after them, but Salmon Jo didn't even turn around. Her grip was unrelenting.

"I went to get you at Panna Stencil Pavlina's," Salmon Jo said. "But I saw her talking to a Doctor, so I ran. I'm so glad I found you!"

"I need to pack a bag!"

"No time. And leave your screen. They might be able to track us with it."

Rubric took out her screen, which she used to draw, take pictures, pulse, make calls, read, watch edfotunement, and tell the time. It was flashing red, pulsing, *Rubric report to Panna Lobe's office at once.* She placed it carefully on the hallway floor. It was the strangest feeling, like she was leaving one of her eyes behind. They ran down the stairs and out the door.

It was odd to be running through the tree-lined campus, the handsome redbrick buildings glowing in the sun, the students lounging on the lawns, and to feel her heart pounding in her chest. Everything around her seemed so normal. But she felt like an animal trying to escape.

"Ah, the library," Rubric said as they arrived at the small white building. "Just where I was expecting us to go. What's going on?"

They swiped their cards and smiled grimly at the Security Klon.

Salmon Jo steered her toward two terminals that were slightly hidden behind a potted plant. They entered their identity numbers. "Pick something plausible," Salmon Jo told her.

What did that mean, plausible? Rubric selected a recent episode of *Who Shall Be My Schatzie?* Then they left the terminals and ran downstairs.

Rubric thought it made sense when Salmon Jo took her into the utility tunnels in the basement. But she was confused when she led her to a door to the Geothermal Pump marked *Staff Only Please.*

"Salmon Jo, they photograph who goes in and out of these doors," she said. She pointed at the scan camera.

"Good," Salmon Jo said.

She opened the door, setting off a tinkly alarm no louder than a wind chime. The Geothermal equipment took up only a tiny part of the room. There were stacks of mysterious rectangular objects that might have been paper books or other historical artifacts, all covered in drop cloths. Before Rubric even had time to really think this, Salmon Jo climbed onto a teetering pile of the artifacts and unhooked a transom window that was over a boarded-over door. Like a gecko, she slithered up the wall and hooked one leg through the window. "Come on, Ru!"

Rubric clambered onto the wobbly stack of artifacts. She handed her arm up to Salmon Jo, who pulled with a mighty grip as Rubric climbed up to the window in an incredibly undignified fashion. She kicked, scattering rectangular artifacts that fell to the floor with a dusty thump. She finally got one leg over the window, and Salmon Jo hauled her up.

"Urgh," grunted Rubric, as she practically knocked Salmon Jo out the window on the other side. Salmon Jo fell lightly to the ground, and Rubric threw her other leg up to the window. Rubric had never felt more ungainly in her life. She slithered down the other side of the wall, collapsing in a heap on the floor. They were back in the steam tunnels.

"Can I stand on your back?" Salmon Jo asked. "I need to shut the window. I'm trying to cover our tracks and throw them off the scent."

Rubric knelt down, and Salmon Jo stepped up on her lower back, heels digging into Rubric's kidneys. "Okay, done." She hopped off.

Salmon Jo led them to another part of the steam tunnels, where there was a padlocked door. There were no cameras here. Salmon Jo hauled a lock clipper from her jacket. She snipped the lock, and they opened the door. Blinking, Rubric followed her out into the sunlight. They were on some sort of disused loading dock.

"Why were you looking for me at Stencil Pavlina's?" Rubric asked. "There was a Doctor talking to her?"

"First of all, I got a visit from a Doctor too," Salmon Jo said, jumping off the dock. "She brought me to her office." She pulled a bag out from under the dock and hoisted it onto her shoulder. "This is some camping stuff. I stored it here last week, just in case. I should have just left it in my room, maybe. It's possible I overplanned this."

They started up the slope away from the library, and Rubric knew they were taking the shortest diagonal route off campus.

"It's okay. Just tell me about the Doctor. What was she like?" Rubric couldn't help asking.

"She was my Jeepie Similar! She was so smart, really smart. I never met anyone so smart. Wow, she looked good in that saffron-colored robe. She was taller than me or Panna Madrigal and kind of queenly looking. She said she had heard that I was spreading a lot of rumors about the origins of Klons. She said ideas like ours sometimes floated through Society. She used the words *legend* and *myth*."

"Like a unicorn," Rubric said.

Salmon Jo gave her a funny look.

"So the Doctor was saying we're wrong?" Rubric asked hurriedly.

"She started out like that. But then she said something like, 'Legends sing of both fact and fiction,' and she quoted something in Latin. She said, 'Only the most intelligent people can handle this information about the Klons. We need people who understand the truth about how Society works. People like that run Society, but they have to be loyal and have the right attitude. For really intelligent people like us, there's not just the Golden Rule, there's also the Iron Rule.'"

"The Iron Rule! What's that?"

"Protect the Doctors, who wield knowledge wisely, and reveal nothing that could be misinterpreted by the populace."

"Misinterpreted," Rubric muttered in disgust. "That's not from some ancient text of wisdom, like the Golden Rule is. They just made that up. It's not even well written."

"*Sssh,*" Salmon Jo said. They were walking fast past a group of girls who were talking and laughing. "Act normal."

Rubric didn't know how to act normal. What was normal when they were fleeing? Salmon Jo didn't look normal. Her skin was ashen except for red spots on her cheeks, and she was practically trembling with anxiety.

"I wonder how she found out what we were thinking," Salmon Jo said. "Panna Lobe must have told."

"Or maybe Nanny Klon did," Rubric said. "She was replaced by a new Nanny Klon today."

Salmon Jo whistled. "Wow. Could be either one of them. Or both. In retrospect, maybe we shouldn't have gone yapping to everyone."

A girl from Yellow Dorm waved at Rubric, and she waved back uncertainly. "So what did the Doctor do next?" Rubric demanded.

"I thought I was in real trouble, but the Doctor started saying all these nice things to me. She asked did I want to be trained to be a Doctor myself, and that someone like me could really help Society."

They had reached the outskirts of the campus. Here was Salmon Jo's favorite tree. She liked to sit in there and think and stare out over the wall at the city. For the first time, Rubric realized you could climb from the tree to the brick wall that surrounded the campus. They were only about a hundred paces from the handsome arch with a wrought-iron gate, where a Security Klon sat, that was the entrance to the campus. Great, more climbing, Rubric thought. The Security Klon never even looked their way as they inched up the tree and over the wall. Rubric began to feel a little better. Everything was so relaxed and trustful in Society, maybe it wouldn't be that hard to be a fugitive.

When Rubric jumped off the wall, she could feel the thud travel all the way from her feet up her spine. They walked quickly down the street, away from the trolley stop that Rubric usually took to Stencil Pavlina's.

"I'm not seeing the mortal danger yet," Rubric said. "They just want to recruit you."

"I asked the Doctor about you," Salmon Jo said. "I wasn't sure if I should. I thought maybe they didn't know about you. Then I thought, who am I kidding? If they know about me, they know about you. Or do you think I did the wrong thing?" Salmon Jo squeezed Rubric's hand anxiously.

Rubric really wanted Salmon Jo to keep her cool. Otherwise she might lose it herself. "It's fine, S.J.," she said. "I think you did right. What did the Doctor say?"

"She asked me how close I was to you. Everything else she said was totally clear and confident. But that one thing was a bit tentative. Then suddenly, she was like of course you could become a Doctor too. But…Ru, I think she was lying."

Rubric laughed. "I know I'm not Doctor material. I don't want to be one of those slave merchants. My Jeepie Type is a visionary, not a bureaucrat. So then what happened?"

"Then nothing happened. She thanked me and told me to think about it. I left. And there were a bunch of Klons in blue robes in the waiting room outside her office. Just like the Klons who came to take Hollyhock away. And then I knew."

"Oh, scheiss!" A Panna they were passing on the street frowned at Rubric. "They were going to give me treatment. They were going to come get me. That's what they want to do."

Once when Rubric was small, she had gone ice skating on a pond with her dorm. The ice had cracked, and she had plunged right through. It had happened so fast. One moment she was skating happily, the next she was churning and choking in the frigid water. Her Nanny Klon had rescued her. Rubric had lain on the ice, teeth chattering, cold and surprised. That was exactly how she felt now.

CHAPTER THIRTEEN

Salmon Jo's plan was to hide out on Mt. Sileza. Rubric was afraid they would have to walk there, and it was several klicks away. But Salmon Jo had figured out a way to take a trolley without having to swipe their cards. "I've noticed that on about ten percent of the trolleys, the card reader is broken, and the Conductor Klon just waves you on. The system seems very poorly maintained. So all we have to do is wait for a bus where the card reader is broken. It shouldn't take too long. We just have to try to remain inconspicuous."

Rubric wasn't sure if she could do that. She was shivering and it wasn't from cold—she was wearing a thick, long-sleeved woolen cloak—but from pure fear. It was really sinking in that they were on the run. Part of her mind kept insisting the whole thing must be some terrible mistake. This part tried to soothe her and tell her everything was fine. But the other part of her mind kept going over what Salmon Jo had said, evaluating and reevaluating it. The conclusion was the same every time: FREAK OUT!

She might never return to Yellow Dorm or see her friends. Never fulfill any of her dreams: to display art, have glam parties, be an amazing mentor to young Jeepie Similars, have a key-exchanging ceremony with Salmon Jo, live in a big house with her, help Salmon Jo invent an airship. But the death of those dreams wasn't even the problem. If they got caught, she would get treatment. She had seen Klons who had been through treatment who were fit for only the simplest tasks because their brains had been totally fried, and they couldn't remember how to do complicated things.

At worst, she would be compost.

Other people were chattering and carrying on with their activities and getting on the trolleys. She and Salmon Jo were the only ones who stayed at the steel-and-glass shelter. Trolleys came and went, and none of them had broken card readers. This fretted Salmon Jo incredibly. She kept muttering stuff about how she was sure her calculations were correct and it didn't make sense. She kept rejiggering some figures in an incredibly boring way. It was driving Rubric up the wall, but she knew that was how Salmon Jo was keeping a grip on things. She nodded and yessed her when necessary. Privately she wondered if this was even necessary. Would anyone try to track them through their cards?

The seventeenth trolley had a broken card reader. It wasn't going directly to Mount Sileza, but nearby. Neither of the girls wanted to wait any longer, so they took it. By the time they finally arrived at the foot of Mount Sileza, it was only an hour before dusk. Everyone they encountered was leaving.

Rubric was tired before she started hiking, mentally tired. The path took many winding switchbacks. The season was turning to autumn, and slippery leaves covered the trail, so Rubric had to stare at her feet as she went. Salmon Jo was much more light-footed—did the girl have radars in her feet? She was looking around her at the scenery instead of down at the path.

At times, they were on level ground and walking was easy. At other times, it was quite steep. Rubric plodded along without complaint, but she kept mentally projecting toward the end of their journey. They would be sitting snug and cozy in a tent, and Salmon Jo would crack out the food. Something really good, like chocolate-covered peanuts. Then Rubric would snap back to herself and realize she was still laboring up some incline and she felt like keeling over. She wondered if she was losing her mind. They stopped to drink some water, and Rubric felt much better. *This isn't so bad,* she told herself. Then realized they weren't moving and that's why it felt so easy.

"Isn't this beautiful?" Salmon Jo said and sighed.

Rubric forced herself to actually look at her surroundings. The last time Rubric had been here, during the annual outing, it had been the height of summer. The trail had been surrounded by dense greenery. Now, most of the foliage was gone, and she could look through the trees and down the mountain. In addition to some lakes, she could see the whole city spread out. It looked very sparkly and jaunty from here. She couldn't see their own campus, but she could see another academy's campus. The crown jewel of the city was the hospital, which had been designed to look like a sailing ship from the days of old. All the round buildings, which up close were plain and unremarkable, from here were quite striking. Those were the buildings where Klons were raised, trained, housed, or given treatment. The Karela Bridge hung ethereally over the river, and not far away was Pearl, the art-materials center. Rubric could just barely see the skylines of other cities, other nature preserves. Far off in the distance was a shimmering line that was the fence that separated Society from the Land of the Barbarous Ones.

"Yes, it's pretty," she said grudgingly.

They continued on their way. Rubric felt quite a bit better. She thought maybe she had been dehydrated. But, still, her relief was almost indescribable when she glimpsed the huge boulder that she remembered from her last trip, a landmark that showed they were almost at the summit.

They reached the clearing just as darkness fell. Salmon Jo wrestled the tent—which she had carried the whole way, Rubric realized—out of the bag as quickly as she could. But it was almost pitch dark before they had even unrolled it. She and Salmon Jo didn't have to say anything; they were both aware of how hard it was to set up a tent in the dark. Each held a flashlight in her mouth. Fumblingly, Rubric snapped the almost-weightless poles together and fitted them into the rings. Her entire self was focused on setting up the tent. She and Salmon Jo said only a few short sentences to each other, stuff like, "No, I think it's this one," and, "Can you turn that thingy over?" They worked almost like one organism.

As soon as the tent was up, they unzipped it, crawled inside, and flopped down. Salmon Jo clipped her flashlight to the roof of the tent, but a few seconds later she clicked it off. As Rubric lay there, her eyes began to adjust to the dark, and she could make out the shape of Salmon Jo and see her eyes and her teeth.

"It's so weird that one second the tent isn't up and then the next it is. And suddenly there's an indoors in the middle of the outdoors," Rubric said.

Salmon Jo didn't answer for a long time. Rubric thought she was considering her statement deeply, but when she spoke all she said was, "I'm lying on a huge pointy rock."

Rubric groaned. "Do I have to get up? Do we have to move the tent, the rock?"

"No. Can you rotate like ninety degrees though? Then neither of us would be lying on the rock. No, no, other way."

"Where's the food?" Rubric asked.

Salmon Jo rifled through her bag with one hand, without looking at it, and tossed a packet to Rubric.

Chocolate covered peanuts! Rubric was so happy that tears came to her eyes. She spread her sleeping bag over her like a blanket, planning to crawl into it later, and began eating the peanuts. She could hear Salmon Jo crunching something loudly. It sounded like carrots.

As soon as she was done eating, she was going to thank Salmon Jo for carrying all the camping bags, and bringing her favorite protein-packed bedtime snack, and planning the whole venture and guiding her and having the foresight to get the hell out in the first place. Then maybe she would recite a nature poem to Salmon Jo. But, to her surprise, the next thing that happened was she woke up to a beam of sunlight coming through an unzipped flap in the tent and hitting her in the eye. She was still lying under the sleeping bag with the packet of chocolate-covered peanuts in her hand.

CHAPTER FOURTEEN

Rubric felt filled with energy. She was eager to do something productive after being such deadweight the day before. In addition, she was quite hungry. She found all the oatmeal Salmon Jo had been hoarding and left the tent as unobtrusively as possible, which turned out to be not very. Salmon Jo slept on.

It looked to be quite early, earlier than Rubric had thought. It was maddening to have no timekeeping device. Salmon Jo wore a watch pendant around her neck, but Rubric was used to looking at her handheld screen.

She was sitting on a stump eating oatmeal and gazing at birds in the leafless shrubbery when Salmon Jo emerged. She handed her a spoon.

"Thanks," Salmon Jo said, digging into the oatmeal.

"I hope you weren't planning to hide out on this mountain for the rest of our lives?" Rubric asked.

Salmon Jo shook her head.

"This isn't real wilderness," Rubric said. "People come here all the time. Ranger Klons patrol the mountain. If someone was looking, it wouldn't be too hard to find us."

"We didn't bring enough oatmeal to last the rest of our lives," Salmon Jo said, her voice scratchy from sleep.

"I wouldn't even want to be in the real wilderness anyway. I'd get lost without paths. I don't know how to gather nuts and berries and all that stuff. Probably I'd eat a poisonous mushroom and die."

"There is no wilderness like that," said Salmon Jo. "Not in Society. Maybe outside the fence, where the Barbarous Ones live."

The birds were singing raucously. Rubric wondered where she had gotten the idea that nature was quiet and peaceful. "So what's the plan?" she asked.

Salmon Jo took another spoonful of oatmeal. "First of all, I just woke up maybe three minutes ago. Second of all, I don't really have a plan. Getting here was as far as it went."

Rubric realized she had been depending on Salmon Jo to come up with all the answers for a while now. It was her turn to step up to the plate. "I forgot to thank you for all that. I thought I did, but I was actually asleep."

"Don't mention it," Salmon Jo said, looking down at the pot and stirring the congealing porridge. The tips of her ears turned pink. She was always embarrassed when someone thanked her. It was incredibly cute.

"We need to figure out what our goals are," Rubric said. "To get the truth out about the Klons? To topple Society?"

"Wow, you're really full of pep this morning. I'm not sure if I'd be very good at those things," Salmon Jo said.

Rubric considered. "Probably no two people will be very good at that," she said. "I think we need to get some more recruits."

"There are probably other people like us out there somewhere," Salmon Jo said. "Who know the truth. Although I have no idea how we would find them. I'm picturing hanging a banner off the Karela Bridge: *If you know that the Klons are actually human, come talk to us, except we can't tell you where we are.* What a logistical nightmare."

Rubric laughed.

"I'd like to think we could just tell Filigree Sue and our other friends, but in truth, I don't think they'd care," Salmon Jo said.

"People like us out there somewhere," Rubric mused. An inspiration blossomed in her head. "You know who *are* people like us?"

Salmon Jo gave her a look. Her just-tell-me look. She didn't understand rhetorical questions. Rubric couldn't break the habit.

"Our Jeepie Similars," Rubric said.

"What, like Panna Madrigal? Or, gee, Panna Stencil Pavlina. Please."

"I was thinking Jeepie Similars our age. Our Klons who are our Jeepie Similars. The girls out there who are exactly like us but they're enslaved." Rubric felt a surge of elation. She felt like she had found her purpose in life. The Klons needed her help. "Let's free them!"

"Hmmm," Salmon Jo said. "How is that possible?"

"It's totally possible!" Rubric said. "It's the right thing to do. It's the only choice. Because we are the only ones who know. We have to help our Jeepie Similars!"

"Okay, I hear you," Salmon Jo said. "But how exactly do you propose we do this?"

"First, I guess we have to go to another city," Rubric said, thinking as she spoke.

Most people found it disconcerting to see Klons who were their Jeepie Similars. Populations were planned accordingly, so as to separate the two groups. In their home city, there were probably a couple hundred humans of Rubric's Jeepie Type, but no Klons of her Jeepie Type. While in another city, there would be no humans of Rubric's Jeepie Type, but plenty of Klons. There were exceptions to this rule. Some people ended up moving to a faraway city where there happened to be Klons of their Jeepie Type. And some celebrities liked to have personal Klons who were their own Jeepie Type, but in general that was considered poor taste.

Rubric could remember once watching a tennis match on a big screen with her friends. A scene of the crowd in the stadium was briefly shown, and there had been a Klon selling sausages who looked a lot like Rubric. Everyone laughed and said, "Oooh, Ru, it's you! There's your Jeepie Similar Klon!" It had given her the strangest feeling.

"The only problem will be finding where specifically our Jeepie Similar Klons are," Rubric said.

Salmon Jo smiled. "I found out what a hacker is! It means people who are able to trick systems into giving them information. I bet I have some atavistic ability at this. I need to learn how to hacker. And maybe we need to change our appearances a bit to keep from being apprehended."

Rubric giggled. "In ancient literature, people who disguise themselves always dress up as males."

"We have to be careful when we approach the Klons," Salmon Jo warned. "If we just come right out and say we want to rescue them, they might fink on us."

"Why would they do that? Of course they want to escape!"

"If I were enslaved, that would make me go veruckt. But Klons don't seem veruckt. They seem regular. So they must have some sort of mindset about their lives that allows them to get on with things. It must be just as disturbing for them to find out their worldview is totally wrong."

Rubric remembered Nanny Klon. "I guess we need to find our Jeepie Similar Klons who are disgruntled and ready to pop."

"What job would make you most disgruntled?" Salmon Jo asked.

"I dunno, donating organs."

"That's not a job, that's just on an as-needed basis," Salmon Jo objected. "For me, it would be driving a trolley. I don't even really like being a passenger on a trolley. And the traffic patterns give me a headache."

"Then maybe they don't make your Jeepie Type Klon into a trolley driver," Rubric said.

Salmon Jo lapsed into thought, staring into space.

We just sound like thicko kids, Rubric thought. *We don't know what we're doing. We've hardly left our campus more than a dozen times, we're playing at camping out in the woods, and now we're supposed to travel to other cities and set Klons free without being captured.* The whole thing was ridiculous. She looked moodily at the oatmeal-caked pot. If she left it much longer without washing it, it would be really hard to get the crust off. Rubric had never washed a pot in her life, and she had no idea where there was any water. Maybe she should just go turn herself in for treatment, and then she wouldn't have to worry about the washing up.

Salmon Jo must have been thinking something similar because she said, "I'm not trying to criticize your plan, but I feel hopeless. All our lives, we were wrong about what Klons are. How many other things are we wrong about? I can't trust any of the information I have in my head. I'm supposed to be a scientist! And I fell for all this flimsy propaganda about 'engineered at a molecular level.' What if we go to another city, and the city doesn't even exist? How are we supposed to know what's true and what's not?"

"You really do have a good nose for lies," Rubric told her. "We only figured this out because you kept rabbiting away about some boring numbers. You're an exceptional human being."

"I don't feel like a human being at all," Salmon Jo said. "I feel like I gave up my human-identity card. When I see how people treat the Klons, I feel so mad. And I was exactly the same way until two weeks ago. If I'm not the same person I was, who am I?"

This was a lot of emoting for Salmon Jo. She was usually pretty low-key when it came to discussing her feelings. Rubric put down the oatmeal pot, scooted closer to her, and put her arm around her.

"I feel—what's the word for when you feel like an alien?"

"Alienated," Rubric supplied.

"Yeah, that." Salmon Jo leaned her face into Rubric's neck.

"You're my alien," Rubric said, smoothing Salmon Jo's wavy bangs off her forehead. "Let's be two aliens together. We'll be all right as long as we're together."

She was just saying it to make Salmon Jo feel better, but she felt a weight fall away from her heart. She realized it was true. They might be all alone in the world now, but Salmon Jo was all she needed.

Rubric brought her face level with Salmon Jo's. Their lips met, and the world vanished. They twined their fingers together, and still they kissed. Rubric forgot all their troubles until an early-morning hiker startled them with some witty remarks about young love.

CHAPTER FIFTEEN

R ubric couldn't believe they were back in the city again after all the fleeing they had done.

This was the best plan they had been able to come up with: they would pretend to be artists making a documentary film about Klons. That way, they might be able to talk to Klons alone. For this to work, they needed, at the very least, a camera. Procuring this was Rubric's job. And they needed the locations of their Jeepie Similar Klons. It was Salmon Jo's job to get those.

Rubric was going to requisition the camera at the art-materials center. But she could not use her card. Even if she had been able to, academy students were not given enough rationing credits to be able to requisition an item as dear as a camera. So she planned to impersonate someone else. She had decided to use Society's weaknesses to her own advantage. Klons were trained to be deferential, even obsequious. She would exploit that. And security in Society generally was lax. Rationing-credit fraud was the only commonplace crime in Society, but she thought she could get away with it.

Rubric sailed as imperiously as she could into Pearl. She headed straight for the tech desk. "Bring me a vid camera," she told the Klon at the art-tech desk, in the most high-handed manner she was capable of.

"What kind, Panna?"

Rubric knew from nothing about cameras.

"The most basic model," she bluffed.

"Certainly, Panna." The Klon bent over and rummaged in a cabinet for a scant few seconds before producing a black cube with a round bit at either end. Rubric picked it up and pretended to inspect it but cut her inspection short because she wasn't even sure which way was up. Now that she had seen one, she thought she could make a dummy version and paint it black if she had to.

"This is exactly what I need," she declared. "Put it on my account. I am Panna Stencil Pavlina."

It was possible that Stencil Pavlina was well-known at Pearl. In that case, Rubric's plan was to run.

"Does the Panna need a battery charger?"

Oh. "Naturally! And an extra battery!"

It took the Klon longer to find a battery and a charger. Then she began poking her clunky handheld screen, the basic kind Klons were given if they needed it for their jobs.

"I'm sorry to say Panna does not have enough credits for an extra battery," the Klon said apologetically. "It's more dear than you would think, and everyone is getting fewer rationing credits this month."

"This will suffice, then," Rubric said. She was trying to project aloof and crazed, like the real Stencil Pavlina, but she obviously wasn't doing a very good job because the Klon engaged her in conversation.

"I apologize again. I'm sure you're doing a big project. If you don't mind my asking, Panna Stencil Pavlina, what kind of project are you working on? I hope you don't think it's intrusive, but I love to hear about the different art masterpieces that the patronesses are creating. That's one of my favorite things about my assignment in Pearl."

"Well," said Rubric, wanting a chance to practice her spiel but afraid it would cast suspicion on her. "You might be interested." Her heart ached for this Klon, clearly bright and creative, who had to be happy that she was able to work in the art-materials center when she should be making her own art. The Klon was really cute. She was pale, but her face flushed when she talked. She was zaftig and had long, straight hair.

"I'm actually making a documentary about Klons," Rubric said.

The Klon's face closed. That would be the only word to describe it. The open friendliness that had been evident a second ago was now gone. The replacement expression was guarded, with a false willingness to please.

"It's going to show what makes…um, humans different, um, from Klons, or not so different," Rubric floundered.

"Fascinating," the Klon said. "Your card please, Panna?"

Rubric slapped the pockets of her cloak. "Why, I have left it at home. No matter. I'll bring it next time." She laid one hand casually on the camera.

"I abase myself, but you must know, Panna, that with all the rationing-credits theft lately, I must have your actual card. It's terrible how a few hooligans who don't understand the Golden Rule have spoiled it for all the other Pannas, but that's just how it is. I'll put your things aside, and you can get them another time."

Rubric laughed haughtily. "Nonsense!"

"It's for your own protection, Panna Stencil Pavlina," the Klon said. "Why, just imagine if one of your Jeepie Similars tried to steal your identity! Maybe some young academy student who knew no better."

Rubric felt her overbearing manner begin to crack. She had picked dozens of Centaurea knapweed flowers up on Mount Sileza and decorated her hair with them, a style that only older women wore. But of course she still looked sixteen.

"Call your Kapo Klon then," she said. "She can vouch for me. *She* could tell me apart from my Jeepie Similars! And while she is here, I will certainly complain about your rude and unhelpful attitude. I'll advise her to send you for treatment! You'll speak more respectfully after you come back from treatment. If you can speak at all!"

Was that too over the top? But the Klon was wavering. Rubric picked up the camera and put it under her arm. The Klon frowned and began consulting her handheld screen. Rubric wasn't sure if she should stalk out now. Maybe run. Or wait?

She felt she had missed her tide, when the Klon said, in a completely different voice, "Oh, I do apologize, but it seems I'm going to have to ask the Kapo Klon to come anyway. It seems some tragedy may have befallen one of your Jeepie Similars."

Rubric's heart began to pound hard. Scheiss, scheiss, scheiss! "I don't have time for that!"

"There's a young girl who's your Jeepie Similar who has disappeared along with her schatzie, and it's feared some harm could have happened to them. Schatzie suicide pact or some such. So they want to talk to all their Jeepie Similars."

"That's very sad, but it has nothing to do with me," Rubric said curtly. "I have to leave now." She grabbed the battery and turned.

"Wait, Panna!" the Klon shouted.

Other people turned to look. A short, burly Security Klon with brown hair in two pointy buns on the top of her head, giving her extra height and a diabolical aspect, was approaching. Rubric could get all high and mighty with the first Klon, who would never dare lift a hand to a human, but the Security Klons were actually trained to do that.

Then Rubric saw the one thing that could make the situation worse. The real Stencil Pavlina an aisle away. Frowning at some glass eyes in a box.

"Look!" Rubric shouted. "It's Rubric Anne, the girl who is missing!" She pointed straight at Stencil Pavlina, who looked up, deeply confused, as well she should be. The Security Klon changed direction and lurched toward Stencil Pavlina, who had a deer-in-headlights expression. Rubric ran past her, out the door, elbowed through the crowd and down the steps, and fled across the street.

Rubric was a polite girl, and she had never pushed and shoved before. Despite her fear, she felt a surge of pure happiness, as if what she had been waiting for all her life was to knock over women carrying packages.

"Watch it!" snapped one Panna.

"Oof! They should discontinue that Jeepie Type!"

Rubric kept on running. She jumped on through the rear door of a trolley and leapt off again a block away, before the Conductor Klon could even open her mouth. She had no idea she was capable of such coordinated athleticism. Finally she came to her senses and realized she had left Pearl far behind. A Security Klon could very well stop her now just for being a rude menace. She slowed down.

She was so overheated that her skin was prickling all over. She took off her cloak and then her tunic, but she still felt like she was boiling. Luckily, she had arranged to meet Salmon Jo at the Singing Fountain. The Singing Fountain was a great meeting place for schatzies, as its many plashing arcs of water created a romantic atmosphere. Although it was usually crowded, people were too focused on their own love affairs to stare at other couples. But right now, Rubric wished she could dive into the water. She was splashing water on her forehead when she heard Salmon Jo's voice behind her.

"We agree not to attract attention to ourselves, and I find you topless, using a historic monument for a bathtub?"

Rubric grinned and turned. Salmon Jo looked tired and still a bit grubby from camping. She was starting to look like a Klon. But her golden eyes were very lively. She gave Rubric a greedy kiss, and her mouth was pleasantly cold. She took Rubric's cloak and wrapped herself in it.

"How is it that you are freezing?" Rubric asked. "It's like summer again today."

"I was hiding in the zygote freezer for the longest time," Salmon Jo said. "Guess what? It turns out that—"

"They're questioning our Jeepie Similars, I know, I know," Rubric said wearily. "How did you get away?"

Salmon Jo bit her lip and looked down at her feet. "I had to clock the Security Klon and run away," she admitted. "A really nice Klon—*woman*—who was always real sweet to me. She knew me. I thought she wouldn't be on shift, but she swapped with someone else."

"It's okay," Rubric told her, rubbing her shoulder. "You had to do it. There's no such thing as a bloodless coup."

"What does that mean?"

"I've read that phrase in old texts. It means when you smother your enemies instead of something bloody."

Salmon Jo looked at her. Salmon Jo usually had a very self-contained expression. A lot of times when Rubric looked at Salmon Jo, she couldn't tell what she was thinking. But when Salmon Jo did stare into her eyes, her gaze was so direct and open and unguarded that it was almost too much. Rubric didn't look away.

"You had to do it," she repeated. "It really is okay." Salmon Jo smiled at her in a watery way.

"So I guess you weren't able to get anything," Rubric said. Without knowing where they should go, a vid camera wasn't much help.

Salmon Jo's smile broadened a little bit. From her pocket she pulled an orange handheld screen with holograms of dolphins on it. A puff of frost flew off it.

"This is Tensility's," she said. "She coordinates with other cities' Hatcheries about what Jeepie Types to create, so I figured she would have good information on her screen. She has a bunch of different screens, and she's *real* absentminded. It might be days before she realizes it's stolen, not mislaid. While I was in the zygote freezer I practiced my hackering skills. Did you know there's an extinct kind of whale that is really a dolphin, called an orca? Anyway, that's her password. I got some of the locations of some of our Jeepie Similar Klons in Velvet City."

Rubric squealed and did a little jumping dance. Some Pannas who were walking by smiled at her. "I got the camera and the battery. I had to run out, but I think it was fine. I wish I could have gotten a second battery. It's always a pain when you're filming and then you have to pause to plug in."

"Ru, it's just a prop. It doesn't matter. It doesn't even have to work."

"If we're going to be holding a camera, we might as well be filming."

"You know we're not really making a documentary, though," Salmon Jo said. Now she looked worried. "Ru, if this is going to work, you have to focus. We are doing one thing—freeing Klons!"

Rubric thought Salmon Jo was talking too loudly in a public place. Then she reflected that it wouldn't matter if anyone overheard her. In Society, the phrase *freeing Klons* was nonsensical. It was like saying *having a conversation with rats* or *playing a song on the zucchini squash.*

"Yeah, yeah, sure," Rubric reassured her. Salmon Jo was such a worrier. "It's just that the documentary is such a great idea too."

CHAPTER SIXTEEN

"Gee, no one has ever asked me that before, Panna," the Kapo Klon said. She was practically wringing her visor in her hand out of nervousness. "I better be asking our Panna, the manager. This is something for a human to decide. Is that okay? I'll be right back."

"Certainly, Kapo Klon," Rubric said politely. It was a freakishly hot day, so the sweat pouring down the back of her neck probably didn't seem strange. A week after they had stolen the vid camera and the handheld screen, they were standing in an eth-fruit farm just a few klicks outside of Velvet City. It had been a week of stealing: stealing electric bikes, stealing pies from windowsills in rural areas where there were no Comfort Stations, stealing clothes from lines. Now, Rubric was ready to steal a Klon. She and Salmon Jo were standing under the blazing sun in a huge field filled with row after row of eth-fruit trees.

The Kapo Klon walked off, hoisting her cylindrical stun baton over her shoulder. The group of Klons in the area immediately slowed their pace. They were picking eth fruits and dropping them into mesh sacks.

"I like this documentary thing already," one Klon said to another, loud enough for Rubric to hear. Her companion laughed. The first Klon straightened up and pushed her visor off her forehead. She pulled her tunic by her collar and wiped her face, revealing a slice of tummy about ten shades lighter than her sun-reddened arms and face. One by one, most Klons dropped their sacks and went to the water trough to drink and dunk their heads. Some flopped right down on the ground. But a few continued working, radiating disapproval to the others. Off in the distance, Rubric saw oxen pulling plows, led by other Klons.

Rubric heard the whine of an electric vehicle. Most of the Klons returned to work. A few seconds later, a little blue vehicle came over the hill into view and parked. The Kapo Klon asked the human manager something, and the manager replied with a curt shake of her head. Rubric had seen that gesture dozens of times from Salmon Jo. With a shock, she realized the manager was Salmon Jo's Jeepie Similar. Rubric and Salmon Jo exchanged glances.

The manager had many long braids. She looked weather-beaten and about fifty years old. As she walked closer, Rubric saw that she limped a little, and there was something not quite right about her face.

"Hello, I'm Castle Mattea," she said in a rougher, more mature version of Salmon Jo's voice. Then a happy grin split her face. "How wonderful! How wonderful! I love to see my little Simmies!"

She embraced Salmon Jo. Salmon Jo was smiling too and returned Castle Mattea's hug. Since Salmon Jo wasn't much of an actor, Rubric figured it must be genuine. They introduced themselves, with fake names.

"So you girls are making a documentary?" Castle Mattea asked. "I'm surprised. Our Jeepie Type is typically not artsy."

"It's really her project," Salmon Jo said. "I'm just helping my schatzie."

Castle Mattea smiled. *If she says anything about how she once had a schatzie of my Jeepie Type, I'll puke on her,* Rubric thought. Stanky older women on the trolley had given her that line.

But Castle Mattea didn't say anything like that. She said, "I want to help you. But this can't be one of those movies about how conditions for the Klons aren't good enough. I'm going to show you our operation here. We do everything perfect, and I have nothing to hide."

"It's absolutely nothing like that," Rubric said. "We really only want to interview Klons who are our Jeepie Similars."

"I'm going to show you the living quarters here, just in case," Castle Mattea said doggedly, in a way that was familiar to Rubric. She brought the girls in the electric vehicle to a concrete building. Inside, the building was just like a dormitory, except there were no doors on any of the rooms. Everything was clean and recently painted. Except for a certain sterility, there was nothing to complain about here. Castle Mattea led them through the hallway, and Rubric saw that each room was different, some messy, some tidy and prim. Some had a single cot, others had two cots shoved together, which took up most of the room. A few had no cots. Most had some sort of decoration on the wall. Some, graphics of popular edfotunement celebrities, others had homemade art on the wall featuring found objects. Parts of the eth-fruit tree were displayed prominently in the art: leaves, stems, flowers, and even dried eth fruits were woven in. There was a great use of duct tape, staples, and string.

"Can I film some of this?" she asked. This Klon art would be an amazing addition to the documentary that she wasn't really making.

"Sure, go ahead," said Castle Mattea. "I keep telling them they have to take that scheiss down, that it's a fire hazard. But they don't listen to me." She showed them a spotless kitchen and a tiny shower room that was being cleaned by one of the Klons. "See? It's like I said. They have nothing to complain about. If they want to couple up with each other, they can. Play loud music after work, they can. If they get injured on the job, they rest up. No one interferes with them and there's no violence. I try to get them a special treat just about every week, like edfotunement or a dessert. I've had to send less than a dozen for treatment the whole time I've been here, and a couple of them even came back. I know each one individually. Sometimes the Kapo Klon gets a bit overzealous with the stun baton, but it's better if I take a hands-off approach. It's just their way, the Kapos, to be very strict. If I keep doing a good job here, I could become a managers' manager. I bet you didn't even know that existed! They report directly to the Doctors."

"I'm impressed with the whole setup," Rubric lied. Actually, the Panna's smug attitude made her sick to her stomach. She was patting herself on the back for not being brutal? "The Klons are clearly being treated very humanely. Can we do an interview now? This is going to blow the art world wide open."

"Sure, sure," Castle Mattea said. She hesitated and then said to Salmon Jo, "It's nice to see a little Simmie like you on the right track. Don't ever get confused and do anything veruckt. It's very important. You have to be a get-along girl and don't make any trouble. You could be a Doctor someday! It's not so bad being a manager. But it wasn't my dream. You could do better."

"I'll keep that in mind," Salmon Jo said expressionlessly.

Castle Mattea led them back outside. Rubric had to admit, the farm was beautiful. Wide open space, bucolic views. As they were driving back to the eth-fruit field, a flock of birds flew by. Rubric was startled to see that the birds were a red metallic color, except for their undersides, which were white with silver flecks. As they wheeled and turned in the sky, following their leader, they made pretty sparkling patterns.

"I've never seen birds like that," Salmon Jo said. "What kind are they?"

"They're Castle Mattea Birds. I invented them. I have a hobby lab here, down by the waterwheel, that I've built up over time to be quite good. I did a bit of genetic tinkering on some local birds. I feed them, so they always stay in the area. Actually, the metallic red was the easy part. The white-and-silver undercarriage took seven generations. Let's just say some of the failures were not pretty."

"And you say our Jeepie Type doesn't become artists," Salmon Jo said. This seemed to please Castle Mattea.

The Klons had spread out, working on different eth-fruit trees. Mattea seemed to know who was where, and she led them to a grove where Rubric immediately saw her Jeepie Similar Klon. Just Rubric's age or maybe a couple years older. Sweating, picking fruit, looking bored. It felt to Rubric like she was looking into the mirror, except this girl had a low-maintenance buzz haircut and a bit of a sunburn. And Rubric had never picked fruit or done any other kind of manual labor in her life. The girl startled when she saw Rubric.

"Picker Klon, these Pannas need to interview you. Be cooperative and truthful with them, and I might have something nice for you at breakfast time tomorrow." Then she leaned back and folded her arms.

Rubric wanted to be alone with the Klon but didn't know how to ask Castle Mattea.

Salmon Jo solved the problem. "Actually, Panna Castle M—"

"Please! Just Castle Mattea."

"I'd be very curious to learn more about those birds, so I was wondering if you could show me while my schatzie interviews the Picker Klon."

Castled Mattea beamed. She led Salmon Jo off, talking excitedly.

Rubric cleared her throat. The other Klons had melted away. She wished Salmon Jo could help her with this. "So you probably noticed that you and I are Jeepie Similars."

"Yes, Panna." The Klon crossed her arms. Okay, there was another difference. This girl had a lot more muscle definition in her arms.

"That's what my project is about. Can I ask you some questions?" Her voice sounded totally phony to herself. She had no idea how to talk to Klons like they were human. She had no practice.

"Yes, Panna."

"First of all, what is your name?"

The Klon's expression was unreadable. "I'm Picker Klon," she said.

"But don't you have a name that you Klons use among yourselves, to tell each other apart?"

"We tell each other apart just fine," Picker Klon said.

"Okay," said Rubric. This wasn't going so well.

"Can I ask you a question, Panna?"

"Please do."

"Shouldn't you turn your camera on?"

Rubric flushed. "This is just sort of preliminary. Would you like to look at the camera?"

"Yes, Panna," she said, looking pleased. "I'd like that very much."

Rubric handed the camera over to Picker Klon. Picker Klon did just what Rubric had done when she first got it, turned it over and over, trying to figure which end was up. She held one end up to her eye, and then the other. Reluctantly, she handed it back to Rubric.

What could she do to show she was an ally before just blurting everything out? Rubric plucked a few eth fruits and threw them on the ground. She pulverized them under her foot.

The expression on Picker Klon's face didn't change, but there was a subtle shift, as though there was an expression behind her expression. Which was disgust. Rubric had the sensation of seeing herself through Picker Klon's eyes. A dissolute, spoiled Panna, cloddish enough to destroy the eth fruits which were the foundation of Society's energy supply.

How could two people be genetically identical but so different that they couldn't communicate?

No. Picker Klon couldn't be expected to read Rubric's mind. Rubric hadn't told her anything.

"What's really going on here, Picker Klon, is my schatzie and I discovered something really ghastly that happens in the Hatcheries. You know how it's supposed to be that entities like me are human and entities like you are not human?"

Picker Klon nodded. "I'm called a Klon, Panna," she said, as if talking to a half-wit.

"It turns out there's no difference, biologically speaking, between me and you. The Doctors don't do anything special to the Klons to make them not human. As far as we can tell, they select some of the Hatchlings to be designated human and the rest to be Klons."

Picker Klon raised one eyebrow. Rubric often did that. It looked good.

"Do you believe me?" Rubric asked.

"To me," Picker Klon said in a hoarse voice, very different from the way she'd been talking up to now, "what you're saying doesn't make any difference. I'm not even sure I know what biology is. And I don't care whether I'm a human or identical to you. But I know my own worth. I know I'm as good as a human and I deserve everything you have. I don't care what the official story is. You still haven't turned your camera on, Panna."

Wow. All her life, people had been calling Rubric impulsive and idealistic, and now she finally understood why.

"Okay," said Rubric. "So the thing is, my schatzie and I are traveling around Society, and we want to free our Jeepie Similar Klons."

The eyebrow raised again. "Free? Are you coming to take me to the Barbarous Ones?" Picker Klon asked in a low voice.

"The Barbarous Ones?" Rubric echoed, confused. "No. Why?"

"Oh." Picker Klon looked equally confused. "I thought... Sorry, what is your plan exactly?"

"To take you away from here, so you don't have to pick eth fruit any more," Rubric said.

"Uh-huh. And then where are we going?" Picker Klon asked.

"We haven't worked that out a hundred percent yet," Rubric admitted. "You're the first Klon on our list. We were just going to play it by ear."

They stared at each other. Then at the same time, one flatly and one apologetically, they said, "It's not much of a plan."

"I would be willing to go with you if you take me to the Land of the Barbarous Ones," Picker Klon said.

"Why do you want to go there?" Rubric asked.

Picker Klon rolled her eyes. "Believe me, I don't, not really," she said. "But I have my reasons. And not a whole lot of options. So are you ordering me to go with you?"

"Um, what?"

"Are you ordering me to go?"

"No," Rubric said.

"Well, Panna, not to put words in your mouth, but maybe you could order me to go," Picker Klon said.

Rubric didn't know if her brain could absorb any more confusion. Might her brain actually explode and drip out through her ears? *Girl's Head Explodes*, in the dark style of Stencil Pavlina.

"You see, Panna," Picker Klon explained patiently, "if I get caught carrying out this lunacy, the penalty for Klons leaving their posts is very severe. So I'm thinking, if this was a case of you ordering me to do something, it is naturally my job to carry out orders from a respected Panna. If your orders turn out to be contradictory to the wishes of other Pannas, then that would be your responsibility."

"Ah. I see," Rubric said. "Picker Klon, I order you to accompany me to the Land of the Barbarous Ones. What I want you to do is sneak away from here and meet me and my companion outside the perimeter of the farm, as close to the entrance gate as you can without attracting attention. Can you do that?"

"Yes, thank you, Panna." She shot off in the direction of the Klon dormitory.

Sweating more than ever, Rubric rejoined Salmon Jo. They took their leave from Castle Mattea. "So?" Salmon Jo asked as soon as they were out of earshot.

"Picker Klon is coming with us," said Rubric.

"Wow," Salmon Jo said, and swallowed. "You know, I'm not sure I really believed this could work."

"But she wants to go to the Land of the Barbarous Ones."

"Good gravy. Why?"

"Don't know. She said she has some purpose for it."

Salmon Jo shrugged. "We have to go somewhere."

CHAPTER SEVENTEEN

They didn't have much parley with Picker Klon until they were sitting around the campfire. Picker Klon said she had never slept anywhere except in a dormitory, so she simply watched with interest as Salmon Jo set up the tent while Rubric made the fire and dinner. Rubric had discovered she had a wonderful talent for building blazing fires, so she was always in charge of this.

They ate quickly without speaking. Salmon Jo, who polished her food off first, poked the fire and said, "I think we're just one day's ride from the fence that separates us from the Land of the Barbarous Ones. But I don't know if there's a place that's better than any other to cross it."

"Klons say that near the town of Lvodz is the best place," Picker Klon said. "I don't know if that's true. Klons escape, but they never come back. So we don't know what happens to them. My schatzie escaped two years ago. The Kapo Klon said she was captured and redistributed. But they would have to tell us that, whether it was true or not. I mean, they want us to think escape is pointless."

"Do a lot of Klons escape?" Salmon Jo asked in surprise. "I never heard that before."

"Of course you wouldn't hear that," Rubric said. "That would imply that Klons don't like their lives and have something to escape from." Rubric felt self-conscious talking to Picker Klon. Every second, she couldn't help thinking that Picker Klon was a Klon, a Klon, a Klon. She wanted to think of Picker Klon as just another girl, but she didn't know how to shake off sixteen years of training. She kept wanting to prove to Picker Klon that she thought she was a real person, even though Picker Klon clearly wasn't worried about Rubric's opinion.

Picker Klon nodded. "We don't escape a whole lot. But it does happen. And there are so many different stories and songs about the Barbarous Ones. Some say they are bestial and they will make you mate with Cretinous Males and, you know..." She made a pregnant belly shape with her hand and crinkled her face in disgust. "Then others say the Barbarous Ones don't really have Cretinous Males or"—she made the pregnancy gesture again— "that these are just stories that Panna humans made up about the Barbarous Ones to make them sound bad. That actually the land of the Barbarous Ones is a wondrous paradise."

"Wow," said Rubric. She felt that brain-exploding thing again and glanced at Salmon Jo. She looked pretty shocked herself. Rubric inched closer to her schatzie.

"I suppose that could be true," Salmon Jo said slowly. "How would we really know?"

"But some of the stories about the Land of the Barbarous Ones being paradise seem too good for true," Picker Klon said. "Like, they say there are trees that grow hot buttered toast with honey, and waterfalls that have vodka instead of water."

"Preposterous," Salmon Jo muttered.

Picker Klon smiled at her. "You *are* like Panna Castle Mattea, except not so cracked up in the head."

It bothered Rubric that Salmon Jo was able to talk to Picker Klon so easily. And Rubric kept thinking about how much *she* had liked Salmon Jo when she had first talked to her and wondering if Picker Klon might feel the same way. Yup, that was a recipe for paranoid thoughts. What if Salmon Jo liked Picker Klon more than she liked Rubric?

"Also, some of the stories say that in the Land of the Barbarous Ones you Pannas will have to wait on us hand and foot while we Klons lie down on the softest pillows and listen to music," Picker Klon told them.

"This is all assuming we can get past the fence," Salmon Jo said severely. Rubric could tell she didn't like the idea of being a slave any more than Rubric did. It seemed none of the stories about the Barbarous Ones mentioned Klons and Pannas living in harmony together. "Should I tell you what I know about the fence?"

"If you would, Panna Salmon Jo," Picker Klon said. "Our stories about the fence are very vague. They say you need special shoes which I don't have."

"First of all, the fence extends fifty feet in the air and is invisible. There's a condenser that's charged by a polycrystalline device—"

"S.J., please, skip the boring part," Rubric asked.

"I am skipping the boring part," Salmon Jo said. "You have no idea."

Picker Klon smiled and ducked her head to hide it. Rubric had never realized how ineffective that strategy was until she saw someone else do it.

"What you really need to know is that the fence itself doesn't exist in a solid state, but when a living thing makes contact with it, they receive an electric shock. Until just a few years ago, the shock was lethal. They had colored flags near the fence to warn people not to wander into it. But deer and elk were always getting cooked. Then a few years ago, there was a rash of human suicides. Lovelorn young Pannas, all copying each other. They put up a big brick wall all along the fence, about fifteen feet high, to stop the suicides."

Picker Klon nodded. "I know someone who worked on that wall. Her back was never the same afterward, and she had to become a Chef Klon, at our dorm."

"The thing was, the locals didn't stop killing themselves. It just became more of a challenge to get over the wall. Now it wasn't lovelorn young Pannas anymore, but middle-aged Pannas. You know how sometimes people have a bit of a crisis, and they get jaded and think their lives are empty and have no meaning?"

"I remember this," Rubric said. She had always been afraid this could happen to her when she became middle-aged. The tales of the bored suicides had been exquisitely painful to her.

"What thickos!" Picker Klon said. "If I were a Panna human, I would never throw my life away."

Rubric bristled. How could her Jeepie Similar be so insensitive?

"They had to change the voltage in the fence to a nonlethal amount," Salmon Jo said. "So that's good news for us."

"Some Klons say the current is off to save energy," Picker Klon said. "Other Klons say the fence is only deadly to Klons because of the chips we wear."

Salmon Jo shrugged. "It depends whether you believe the main point of the fence is to keep out the Barbarous Ones. Either way, they can probably track you down if you're wearing that chip."

"I'm going to slice it out tomorrow morning," Picker Klon said.

"What about tunneling under the fence?" Rubric asked.

"Negative," Salmon Jo said. "They have metal plates underneath the earth all along the fence, to carry the current."

"That's what my friend who worked on the fence said too."

"I wonder if there's a way to turn off one section of the fence," Rubric said.

The others shrugged.

"We'd better go to sleep, so we have the strength for all this slicing chips and jumping walls and getting zapped," Rubric said. She was cross that they had to navigate this dangerous fence and go to the Land of The Barbarous Ones just to please Picker Klon. And it disturbed her how sketchy and contradictory all the information was.

"Okay," said Picker Klon immediately, unrolling the sleeping bag Rubric had lent her. "Dream of butter!"

Salmon Jo smiled. "We say, sweet dreams."

Picker Klon smiled back. "That's sort of my nickname, Dream. Because I'm always having a dream of something better."

Me too, thought Rubric, but she didn't say anything. She crawled into the two-person tent she and Salmon Jo were sharing and hung her flashlight from its ceiling. The tent was starting to smell sort of like a pungent combination of herself and Salmon Jo. She liked it. Maybe they really would live in this tent for ever and ever.

Salmon Jo crawled inside. "I hope she'll be okay out there," she said. "She's never slept outdoors before."

"She'll be fine," Rubric said. She pictured the first night she had ever slept outside, in the front yard of her first dorm, when the Nanny Klons had organized a campout. She had loved gazing up at the stars.

They spread Salmon Jo's sleeping bag over them like a blanket. Rubric snuggled up to Salmon Jo and started kissing her. But after a minute Salmon Jo pulled away. "I don't want her to hear us," she whispered. "It's embarrassing."

"Fine, be like that," said Rubric. She just let her hand rest on Salmon Jo's belly. She was getting skinny.

Salmon Jo sighed and put her face in Rubric's neck. "You know what I wish?"

"What?"

"I wish we could go in the airship you designed. If only we were allowed to have air travel, we could just fly over the fence and go to the Land of the Barbarous Ones that way."

Chapter Eighteen

It was late afternoon of the following day when they arrived at the fence. It had taken them longer than they had projected, mostly because Dream/Picker Klon extracting the chip from her belly had proved to be a more grisly affair than any of them had expected. Salmon Jo said it was normal for the fat on your abdomen to bleed a lot, but Rubric had the impression she was just making that up to calm Dream down. Dream had been very brave, cutting the chip out herself without screaming or crying, but afterward, she threw up copiously.

It was a desolate area, almost desertlike. Salmon Jo said when the fence was put up generations ago, Klons had been told to scorch all the plant life out of the area because if brush touched the fence, it could start a fire. They had to spray the area with pesticide to keep weeds from growing back. And without the plant life, the area experienced soil erosion and became dusty.

Rubric had never been to a place before that was neither settled nor a nature preserve. Despite the emptiness of the landscape, there was something so open and wild about it. They parked the electric bikes, stolen days ago just outside of Velvet City, under a tree near some rubbish that had been left there. They looked moderately inconspicuous, or so Rubric hoped. All their surroundings had an abandoned quality.

"I'm surprised no one guards this border," Rubric said.

Dream snorted. "What would stop Security Klons from taking off, over the wall and through the fence?"

"Yeah, and we Pannas don't want to stand around in the hot sun," Salmon Jo joked.

"There might be occasional patrols, though, so let's be fast," Rubric warned.

The wall that protected the fence was intimidating itself. Rubric remembered how hard it had been to scramble up the wall and out the window in the basement of the library, and this was probably twice as high. Although the wall was only built a few years ago, it looked ancient.

"What about if Dream stands on my shoulders and clambers over the wall?" Salmon Jo said.

"How am I supposed to get on your shoulders?" Dream asked.

"Stand on Ru's back," suggested Salmon Jo. Rubric got down on her hands and knees.

"Sorry, Panna," Dream said and placed a dusty slipper on Rubric's back. There was a period of grinding into her spine, and then Dream was up on Salmon Jo's back. Rubric got up and helped Dream stand on Salmon Jo's shoulders. But, try as she could, Dream couldn't get up to the top of the wall or anywhere near it. Then Salmon Jo's knees buckled, and they were both on the ground.

"I'm sorry," said Dream, panting. "I don't think I can do that. Wow, those bored suicides were in good shape."

It made Rubric feel better to see that Dream was as clumsy as she was. She had been told all her life it was genetic. Clearly, it was.

"It would really help if we had a rope," Salmon Jo said. "I guess we could slice up the tent, but I hate to do it."

"Oh. I have a rope," said Dream. "It's in my bag."

Being a thicko must *not* be genetic, Rubric thought meanly. But she reflected that Dream had actually brought a rope. What had Rubric brought? A vid camera.

Salmon Jo tied knots in the rope every foot or so. She then emptied her own bag, and they all gathered stones. They put the stones in the bag, tied the rope to the heavy knapsack, and tried to toss the knapsack over the wall. The bag turned out to be too heavy. After they took a few stones out, when Salmon Jo stood on Rubric's back, she was able to toss the knapsack over the wall, keeping a tight hold on the other end of the rope. Rubric was tired of being stood on.

Salmon Jo grabbed the rope and pulled herself up. Before she reached the top, the knapsack slithered back over the wall, but Salmon Jo was able to grab the top of the wall. When she swung one leg over, she seemed to lose her balance a little bit, and for a few seconds it looked like she was going to fall over the other side of the wall. But she steadied herself and then raised her arms in a victory pose.

They ferried all their possessions over the wall. Now was the hard part. Rubric and Dream glanced at each other, and for the first time they shared a moment of pure communication. Communication of fear.

"After you, Panna?" Dream asked hopefully.

Salmon Jo dangled the rope down, sitting on it to anchor it securely and gripping it tightly. Rubric stood on Dream's back to give herself a head start and then began to climb the rope.

It was perhaps the most nightmarish experience of her life. Half the time she was just hanging there, but even that was more work than her arms and legs were used to. Pulling herself up to each knot was agony. Once, her feet slipped off the rope knot, and she was hanging by her hands. She began to slide and almost let go. Only the awareness that she would have to do it all again gave her the strength to get her feet back onto the rope and continue shimmying up.

At last, she was high enough for Salmon Jo to grip her under her armpits and help her scrabble to the top of the wall. Groaning, Rubric lay along the wall's narrow top, gripping its sides with her quivering arms and legs. She felt she would be happy to lay there until the end of time.

When she next looked up, Dream was climbing the rope. She looked like a defective snail, writhing her way slowly along. When Dream reached about halfway, she began letting out a string of curses, some of which Rubric had never even heard before, and she didn't stop until Ru and Salmon Jo had pulled the rope up high enough so she could reach the top of the wall.

"Damn this pregnant male scheiss-for-brains wall! I should have brought a ladder!" Dream said and fell off the other side of the wall.

"Are you okay?" Salmon Jo called.

A groan, and then, "Uh-huh!"

Ordinarily, jumping off a wall wouldn't put a song in Rubric's heart. But compared to climbing up, it seemed positively easy. She slithered off the wall and let go. The fall was short.

"How we doing?" Salmon Jo asked softly. "No broken bones?"

Rubric's legs throbbed a little, but she could walk without limping. "I'm okay," she said, and the others echoed her.

"We are so lucky," Salmon Jo said. "For the moment, we're covered in myrtle!"

They picked up their knapsacks. They tried to evaluate the invisible fence before them. Rubric wondered where it was exactly. Then she thought she could see it shimmering, like the air on a very hot day. "When I look hard, I can almost see it," she said. "It's like a translucent rainbow."

"Did you fall on your head?" Salmon Jo asked.

"I don't see nothing," Dream said.

Rubric still thought she could see something shining with a tremulous light. But it was easy to believe she was imagining it. Through the fence, Rubric could see the Land of the Barbarous Ones. Not surprisingly, it looked very similar to the land of Society. In the distance, it became lush and green, but Rubric saw no sign of human habitation.

She realized they had all been staring at the fence for a while.

"So I guess we just run through it," Salmon Jo croaked. She cleared her throat.

Rubric sighed. It was such a low-tech plan.

"Have I mentioned I have a fear of electric shocks?" Salmon Jo said.

"I'll go first," Dream volunteered. "I mean, I am a Klon. I am genetically programmed to do things that could potentially save a human's life."

"No, you're not," Rubric said. "That's not actually true." She was so annoyed that she was able to pelt forward at full speed.

The pain was horrifying. She felt a buzzing in every muscle in her body, hot and yet numb at once. She screamed only a little, a short, strangled shriek. Then it was done, but her heart was beating funny. Could that strange feeling be her very bones aching? Rubric was lying on the barren ground, gasping. She started to feel better as she breathed in air that felt very cold. But the veins in her wrists were throbbing, as if her pulse was trying to escape from her body. She hoped they didn't burst open.

She looked up. Through the fence she could see Salmon Jo and Dream. They looked sort of wiggly. She couldn't tell if it was seeing them through the fence that made them wiggly or if it was her brain being fried that made them wiggly. Maybe she was actually still vibrating inside?

Salmon Jo and Dream didn't look eager to race through the fence. Perhaps watching her go through and listening to her scream had not been inspiring. They were talking. They were close enough that Rubric should have been able to hear them, but she realized there was a ringing in her ears. Then the ringing went away, and Rubric decided she felt basically fine.

"It's not that bad!" she shouted. Salmon Jo and Dream were running toward the fence full tilt. Dream grabbed Salmon Jo's hand.

Rubric knew it wasn't going to be fun to watch them go through the fence, but she wasn't expecting that horrible scream from Salmon Jo. Dream kept running, but Salmon Jo flopped to the ground. Her body was convulsing, shaking so hard her teeth rattled. Rubric scrambled over to her side. Salmon Jo's eyes were wide and staring, but she locked glances with Rubric. She looked terrified. Then her eyeballs rolled back in her head.

"Salmon Jo, Salmon Jo!" Rubric screamed. "Are you all right?" A thicko thing to say. She clearly wasn't all right. Salmon Jo couldn't respond. She touched Salmon Jo's shoulder gently. She smelled piss, and she saw that Salmon Jo had a dark stain on her leggings.

Dream was beside her too. In the background, Rubric thought she saw another figure hurrying toward them, but she had no time to process this information.

"I think she's having a seizure," Dream shouted.

"What do I do?" Rubric said.

"Put a stick in her mouth," Dream said. "She might bite her own tongue off or choke on it."

"A stick?" Rubric couldn't tear her eyes from Salmon Jo's shaking face long enough to look around. "You look for a stick."

Rubric cupped her hand behind Salmon Jo's head. She didn't want Salmon Jo to hurt her head. "It's okay," she told Salmon Jo. It sounded like a big fat lie. "You're going to be fine." She wasn't sure if Salmon Jo could hear her.

Dream was at her side again, waving a stick. Then another woman was there. She looked dirty, like a menial Klon, but spoke sharply and confidently.

"Don't put anything in her mouth," the woman said. "That won't help. She'll stop shaking soon. I know it's scary, but this will be over soon."

It didn't feel soon, but Salmon Jo did stop shaking and seemed more alert. "Just roll her on her side," the woman said. Without waiting for Rubric, the woman gently turned Salmon Jo onto her side.

"What is her name?" she asked.

"Salmon Jo," Rubric said.

"What weird names they have," the woman muttered. "Salmon Jo, you're going to be just fine. This was a seizure you had."

"Can she hear us?" Rubric asked.

"Probably," the woman said. "It's always wise to act as if they can."

"Are you a Doctor?" Dream asked.

"I don't really know what that is, so probably not," the woman said.

For the first time, it struck Rubric that this woman was a Barbarous One.

"Hey, S.J., can you hear me?" Rubric stroked her clammy forehead. "I'm glad you're okay."

"That was brutal," Salmon Jo said thickly. "I think I pissed myself." She stretched a bit and reached for Rubric's hand. Then she closed her eyes.

"She is going to be very tired now and may even take a nap," the woman said. "Don't worry, that's normal. It doesn't mean anything bad. Having a seizure takes a lot out of you."

Dream had taken a cloak from her bag and folded it, and now she put it under Salmon Jo's head for a pillow.

"Is she really going to be okay?" Dream asked in a low voice.

"Most likely," the woman said, even more quietly. "It does sometimes happen that people suffer brain damage. But that's rare."

"I can hear you, you know," Salmon Jo said, without opening her eyes.

Chapter Nineteen

The Barbarous woman had arrived in a little red cart pulled by an animal. Salmon Jo sat in the cart with the Barbarous woman and their bags, while Rubric and Dream walked behind it. The animal—it looked like a small horse, but with long ears like a rabbit—wasn't very fast, but Rubric and Dream did have to walk quickly to keep up with it. Its hooves kicked up dust that went right up Rubric's nostrils, even if she pulled her collar up over her nose. The journey seemed to take forever, and Rubric was dead tired by the time they reached their destination. She barely took in any impression of the village.

The Barbarous woman had introduced herself as Theodorica, and Rubric supposed it was her house they went to. Like the other buildings they had passed, it had incredibly thick walls that seemed to be made of mud, and a low roof with grass and flowers growing on the top.

Rubric had to help Salmon Jo out of the cart. "That was a bumpy ride. Someone needs to pave that road. That quadruped is called a molly," Salmon Jo added, proving that the seizure hadn't stopped Salmon Jo's unquenchable thirst to classify everything she saw.

"Welcome to my home," Theodorica said and made a spiraling gesture with her hands. She said it in a very formal way, and Rubric couldn't tell if she really meant it. "I hope you will enjoy a good night's rest here."

"Salmon Jo and I have a tent," Rubric said. "We can sleep outside." She just wasn't ready to sleep in a Barbarous house.

"That is fortunate," Theodorica said. "I have to stable the molly. Would you like to bathe, Salmon Jo? You've been through a lot."

"Yes, please."

"You others are welcome to bathe as well, but I must ask you not to use too much hot water. We have only a very limited amount. Perhaps you can share the same bathwater?"

What a stingy offer, Rubric thought. "No, thank you," she said. She did not want to be beholden to the Barbarous Ones for anything, not even some hot water.

She set up the tent while Salmon Jo took a bath, and Dream helped Theodorica with the molly. An urgent need led Rubric to the composting toilet, which was in a small outbuilding. It didn't foam like the composting toilets at home; she had to throw sawdust into the toilet. Rubric was pleased she had figured out the strange system and also pleased it didn't smell.

Salmon Jo was stretched out in the tent when Rubric returned. Now that Rubric had peed, a new need that had been masked by the other surged to the fore: she was terribly thirsty. She didn't want to go into Theodorica's house, but she didn't think she could wait until morning for a drink.

"Salmon Jo, where's the kitchen in that house?"

"It's all the way at the back," Salmon Jo murmured. "Theodorica gave me an apple, that's how I know. But there's a back door."

That was exactly what Rubric needed to know. She first searched in vain for a well, which she imagined primitive people would have, and then headed for the back door.

Inside, the kitchen was dark, cool, and surprisingly spacious. A jug of water and some earthenware cups sat enticingly right on the table. Rubric poured a cup, downed it immediately, then poured another.

A shuffling noise made her look up. At the other end of the kitchen, by the unlit woodstove, was a rocking chair. In the chair sat what could only be a Cretinous Male. It was so foreign and repulsive looking that Rubric started, splashing water all over her feet.

The Cretinous Male was taller and broader than any person Rubric had ever seen. It seemed poorly constructed, as though it had no hips or waist. Its cheeks were covered with dark, forbidding stubble. She could see more hair peeking out of the top of its tunic. Even its hands and knuckles seemed to be covered with the bristling hairs. And look—there were hairs in its revoltingly large nose. The throat had some kind of lump in it, like a tumor. In one hand it clutched a toy. The Cretinous Male was staring at her with bright, curious eyes. It shook the toy, which made a jingling noise. Suddenly, the Cretinous Male laughed.

Rubric shuddered and took a step back. The thing that terrified her most was the deep timbre of that laugh. The laugh sounded violent, strong, and—of course—completely cretinous.

The back door opened behind her. Rubric heard Theodorica's voice, but she was too afraid to take her eyes off the Male.

"I see you've met my son, Branknor. Branknor, this is Rubric. Can you say hello?"

"Huh-lo!" Branknor boomed.

Rubric knew it was rude, but she couldn't help herself. She turned and shoved past Theodorica. The door banged shut behind her. In her agitation, she dropped the cup onto the grass as she ran past the house. In one fluid movement she unzipped the tent and dove inside. With shaking fingers she closed the tent behind her.

"There's a Cretinous Male in the house," she hissed.

"What? Where?"

"It's lurking in the kitchen."

"Wow, I've gotta see this," Salmon Jo said. "That's amazing!"

"Salmon Jo, wait. Don't go in there. It's really scary!"

"Don't worry," she said. "And I think they're called *he*."

Rubric left the flashlight on. There was no way she could sleep in the dark, knowing Branknor was in that house only a few yards away. How many others like him were there in this town of horror? She waited and waited for Salmon Jo. She took the longest time, and when she finally came back, her only comment was, "Cool!"

Chapter Twenty

Rubric and Salmon Jo sat on the grass in front of Theodorica's house, eating some kind of porridge for breakfast. Rubric didn't want to go into the house, but Dream was in there, helping Theodorica with some menial task.

"If you're feeling well enough, let's leave right after breakfast," Rubric said. "This whole place gives me the creeps."

"I don't know if I'm ready to face the fence again so soon," Salmon Jo said. "And aren't you even a little bit curious about the Land of the Barbarous Ones?"

Theodorica's house had seemed so isolated and rural, but women were passing by on the dirt road all the time. Now a pretty girl with short red hair was running up to the house. She had a wild look in her eyes.

"Dream?" she asked, reaching for Rubric. She looked like she was about to kiss her.

"No, no, no," Rubric and Salmon Jo yelled. "She's in there!"

The girl ran toward the house, shouting Dream's name.

"Prospect!" Dream ran out, flinging porridge from a wooden bowl as she threw her arms around the young woman. They began to hug and kiss and laugh and murmur to each other. Theodorica came out of the kitchen too, to see what was going on. Dream was standing in her porridge and grinding it into the grass as she stood on tiptoe to kiss the taller girl.

Theodorica walked up to them, her lined face split by a smile, and swatted them with a dish towel. "Go inside, young

lovers. You can have your tender reunion in my sitting room."
The girls went inside, still glued to each other. Theodorica came
and sat down beside Rubric and Salmon Jo.

She started explaining something about how she was
responsible for their welfare because she had been the first to find
them after they crossed the fence. But Rubric stopped listening
when she caught sight of two women walking down the street.
One had her arm around the other's back, supporting her because
she was hugely...*pregnant*. It was the most obscene thing Rubric
had ever seen. The woman was wearing a tunic that rose up on
her swollen, distended belly. Her skin was stretched tight over
her lump of a tummy. It looked like she had swallowed a giant
pumpkin, one that might suddenly explode out. Rubric tore her
eyes from the woman's belly to look at her face. How could she
look so proud and happy when she was using her own body as
a gestation tank? Rubric wasn't sure which was more repulsive,
the Cretinous Male or this pregnant woman. She deeply regretted
the chain of events that had led her to come to this bizarre village.

"Does everyone who lives in your land have to become
pregnant?" Rubric blurted out.

Theodorica smiled. "Your people have many myths about
my people. No one who lives here is forced to bear a child. But
to us, this is the greatest fulfillment a woman can ever have. It is
the cornerstone of our communities and our spiritual beliefs. We
have a strict replacement policy, to control our population, with
the result that not everyone who wants to become implanted with
an embryo may do so."

Rubric was just staggered that women would be vying to
get pregnant, the most disgusting thing in the universe. The
Barbarous Ones were as Barbarous as described.

"Excuse me, Panna Theodorica," Rubric said. "But you say
implanted with embryos. Does that mean no one has to mate with
the Cretinous Males?"

Theodorica's face darkened. "Rubric," she said, "I know
you just arrived in our land, and you know no better. But the first

and most important thing you need to know is we do not call our Sons Cretinous Males. That is a degrading and rude name. When you want to refer to them, you must call them the Sons."

"I'm sorry," Rubric said. But she didn't feel sorry.

"No one mates with our Sons," Theodorica said. "They are in a protected class, like children. I understand that even in your own slave-owning land there are taboos of that kind."

"Of course," Rubric said.

"You will learn the ways of Society," Theodorica said in a softer tone.

"Of what?"

"Society. That's what our country is called."

"But my country is called Society," Rubric spluttered. "Your country is called—" She stopped. The Barbarous Ones would hardly describe *themselves* as barbarous, no matter how true it was.

"We call your country the Land of Our Slave-Owning Neighbors," Theodorica said.

Rubric thought it was thicko to have two countries both named Society. She resolved to keep on calling this place the Land of the Barbarous Ones.

"We are not so different," Theodorica said. "Reflect that we all speak the same language."

Salmon Jo shrugged. "Doesn't everyone?"

Actually, Rubric thought Theodorica spoke a little bit oddly, but she was too polite to point it out.

"No, my dear Salmon Jo. On this vast planet, there are many languages, many ways, many customs."

Rubric and Salmon Jo glanced uneasily at each other. There were more people out there besides the Barbarous Ones?

"I know the size of our planet from studying astronomy, but I thought it was only us left," Salmon Jo said. "No one ever said anything about a land other than ours and the Land of the Barbarous Ones. I thought the human race had died out in all the other places, with the advent of cret—with, you know. The mitochondrial disorder your Sons have."

Theodorica laughed heartily. "No, there are pockets of humanity all around the globe. But don't be ashamed of your ignorance. You were deliberately kept in the dark about so much. Here, you can learn, now that you are no longer enslaved, forced to labor for cruel, selfish aristos."

"Actually, we weren't Klons," Salmon Jo said awkwardly. "We were the cruel, selfish—I mean, we were designated human."

There was a silence. "Indeed? Why, then, are you here?"

"Because we were freeing Klons. Dream is the first one we freed, and she wanted to come here."

"To be frank, I am a little alarmed by what you say," said Theodorica. "We are happy to help escaped slaves because we feel compassion for them, but I don't like the idea of disenchanted aristos coming too. I'm not sure we can absorb many of you. Why can't you stay home and fix your own country?"

"We're not staying long," Rubric said. "We only wanted to escort Dream here."

"I am curious to learn about the Cretinous Males and the biology of how you grow fetuses in yourselves instead of tanks," Salmon Jo said in a rush. "I would love to find out more while I'm here, if you don't mind, Theodorica."

She stared. "You plan to cross the Barrier again?"

"Well, yes. Is there any other way?"

"No, there is no other way. But, Salmon Jo, perhaps you do not realize that those who have seizures once when they cross the Barrier will most likely have them again if they repeat the experience."

Rubric's heart sank. She didn't think she could watch Salmon Jo go through that again.

"Would I...?" Salmon Jo faltered. "Is that, is that guaranteed?"

"I can't say that," Theodorica said slowly. "But it's happened enough times that I can't recommend that anyone who's had a seizure should ever cross again. We have too much experience with seizures here, as many of our Sons have them. You must know there are times when the outcome of a seizure can be fatal."

CHAPTER TWENTY-ONE

Prospect had taken Dream away with her to her home in Hot Buttered Toast Town, a nearby village made up entirely of former Klons. But Rubric and Salmon Jo stayed at Theodorica's. The following morning, Rubric and Salmon Jo were awoken by Theodorica, rapping on their tent poles with a stick. She had come to bring them to work picking apples. She didn't explain why they had to do this. "It's better to get it done before the full heat of the day," was all she said.

The girls sleepily followed Theodorica down a dusty road. Many other women and some Cretinous Males joined them. Their walk ended in a lush orchard. The apple trees were surrounded by beds of flowers, mostly past their prime and wilted, as well as herbs and other plants. A few women were picking from ladders, but most people were just walking around plucking apples and placing them in woven baskets. Some women were leading children and Cretinous Males by the hand. The Cretinous Male children were less disturbing to Rubric than the adults. They looked almost exactly like girls, without the hairiness, gigantism, and strange anatomy that characterized the adults. Most of the male children had spacey expressions or walked with difficulty. Some were in pushchairs. But others were running around, and Rubric only knew they were males by the fact that their hair was unbraided and they wore the same peaked visors as grown males.

Rubric was surprised to see Dream and Prospect arrive, and she made her way over to them.

"What are you doing here?" she asked. "I thought you went to Hot Buttered Toast Town."

"We did," Prospect said. "The two towns share this orchard."

Dream stared about her at the orchard. Rubric could almost see her comparing it to the toast trees of legend.

"I picked enough fruit already," she said. "What's the difference between here and home if I have to pick fruit?"

"Here no one lies idle while others toil for them," Prospect said.

Dream pointed wordlessly at a group of Cretinous Males of all ages lying in the shade, staring at the sky while women fanned them. "They don't eat apples?"

"Okay, everyone who can must pick apples," Prospect amended. "Look at it this way. If we don't pick apples, we have no fruit to eat all winter. Besides, we just work for a few hours a day here. It's a snap."

"Fine," Dream said and started picking.

Rubric began to pick apples. Picking one apple was easy, but keeping on doing it was hard work. Dream and Prospect were like apple-picking machines, filling their baskets twice as fast as Rubric. Beside her was a woman with a teenaged Cretinous Male, probably her son. He picked apples very slowly and kept dropping them, or laughing at nothing. His mother kept rubbing his back and telling him what a great job he was doing. When he laughed, sometimes she did too. Clearly all these people were insane.

Salmon Jo came over to join Rubric. She looked flushed and happy.

"I am so pleased with myself," Salmon Jo said. "I've never done anything like this before. This might be better than running!"

"Maybe you should be taking it easy today," Rubric suggested.

"Actually, I feel great. Guess what, Theodorica was telling me why there are all these other plants around the trees. The flowers attract bees, and there's a kind of plant called artichoke that provides soil-building mulch. She says artichokes are tasty. The Barbarous Ones are trying to create a natural ecosystem in their orchards."

"Fascinating," Rubric said flatly. "You may feel great, but I'm sick of this." She sat down under the tree where Dream and Prospect were working. She folded her tired arms.

Dream laughed at her. "We just barely got started! I bet Theodorica is sorry she got stuck with two lazy Pannas who are allergic to working. Have you even lifted a finger to help her with her chores?"

Then everyone started talking at once.

"They're Pannas?" said Prospect, taking a step back. "Are you kidding me?"

"I'm not lazy," Salmon Jo said. "I'm very energetic. I worked in the Hatchery. They must have some primitive lab here to create the embryos. I could work there. And Rubric is an artist. She could make this town a little nicer looking. Even I can see it could use a little something."

"They're okay," Dream told Prospect. "I wouldn't have been able to escape without them and their electric bikes. They want to be mutinous renegades or something."

"I never thought I would have to look at Pannas again," Prospect said. "And I thought if I did, it would only be to spit on them."

That was too much for Rubric. "Well, don't spit on me. That's thicko. And, Salmon Jo, we're going to be leaving soon. You're not going to have time to work in their lab."

"How is it going to help Theodorica if you work in a lab?" Dream asked.

"Hmm," said Salmon Jo. "Good point. I don't know how to do chores, though."

Dream laughed. "It's not that hard. You might be smart enough to learn. You would have to be better at it than the Cretinous Male. While I was there, I saw her Son mixing a bowl of fruit salad. He's a menace to fruit everywhere. Theodorica could have done it twice as fast if she'd done it herself without him, 'cause she had to help him every minute. And then she was telling him what a good job he did!"

"*Sssh,* not so loud," Prospect said. "That's how they do things here. That's the way it is. They want their Sons to do stuff, even if they suck at it. It's their philosophy."

"That's my clever Prospect," Dream said, her hands still a blur of apple picking. "She understands all about philosophy. Whatever that is. I knew you hadn't really been redistributed, my snuggle bunny. I could feel it in my bones."

"There were lots of other ladies here who were interested in me," Prospect bragged. "But I waited for you. I knew you'd come after me."

They stopped their whirlwind of picking long enough for a sloppy kiss. These two were so happy it was almost disgusting. Dream looked like she was having an otherworldly experience, her eyes just barely slitted open in bliss. Rubric couldn't help wondering if that was what she looked like when she smooched Salmon Jo. Rubric thought it must almost be worth it to be separated if you got back together again in the end.

Just then, a woman blew a trumpet, and everyone broke for a picnic lunch that was spread out for them on a huge blanket. There was chicken, cheese, a cabbage dish, a funny kind of bread, water, lemonade, and cider. Rubric got her food eagerly.

Theodorica joined them. "Do you have enough to eat?" she asked.

"Yes," Rubric said. She was tired of the woman hovering over them. It wasn't Rubric's fault the Barbarous Ones had some veruckt custom about being responsible for people they found.

Rubric watched the Cretinous Males eat. She was getting used to looking at them. Most of them were very pale and wore visors to protect them from the sun. They ate boluses of medicine along with their food, so they must be sick. Some of them were being fanned, so they were either very spoiled or they got overheated easily. And from the languid way they lounged around, they seemed to have no get-up-and-go. One teenaged Cretinous Male was repeating, "I pick apples? I pick apples?" over and over to an elderly woman. She paid no heed to his words and kept encouraging him to drink a vast quantity of watered-down lemonade.

"Panna Theodorica, I'm afraid I'm going to be rude again," Salmon Jo said quietly. "But I'm just trying to understand. Why do you want to keep people who are so damaged perpetuated in your society?"

"We love our Sons," Theodorica said. "Their lives have value. We like having them around. Taking care of them makes us better people. We don't think we're better than our Sons, and we don't want to obliterate them. Our only consolation when they die is that another of their icon—what you call Jeepie Type—will be born. It's so obvious that I don't know how to explain it to you. I always hope that when newcomers meet our Sons, everything will become clear to them. If you are going to live here, you have to display tolerance, at the very least. We didn't ask any of you to come here."

The Barbarous Ones didn't want them here, and Rubric didn't want to be here. On that, at least, they could all agree. She didn't understand why she and Salmon Jo were wasting time picking apples when they should be working on how to pass back through the fence safely.

Dream and Prospect invited them for a post-apple-picking party in Hot Buttered Toast Town that night. Hot Buttered Toast Town was only a couple of klicks away. Superficially, it was exactly like the Barbarous village, with the same style of cottages. The wonderful difference was they didn't have to worry about seeing any scary Cretinous Males or pregnant women.

Rubric was worried that the Klons there would be angry at them for being Panna humans, but that wasn't the case. Everyone seemed to accept them as being on the right side. Rubric almost felt like an honorary Klon. It was funny, she would have thought they would stop calling themselves Klons, but they seemed to like the name. The party naturally devolved into a strategy session about how Society could be overthrown and all the Klons freed. Rubric felt she didn't know enough to contribute to the conversation, but she found it very interesting.

At first, she felt joy. This was the group of comrades she and Salmon Jo had been looking for. Wasn't this why they had decided to free Klons in the first place? Maybe coming to the Land of the Barbarous Ones had been worth it.

But soon her emotions gave way to uncertainty. The biggest problems that the Buttered Toast Rebels had to overcome were their small numbers and the oath of nonviolence they had pledged to the Barbarous Ones.

"But, at some point, we're going to have to stop taking that oath seriously," said an intense blond-haired woman named Shade. "The Barbarous Ones have helped us, but our first loyalty is to our own people. Who are imprisoned, who are exploited, who are slaving fourteen hours a day for scum, who are treated worse than animals, whose lives are being thrown away in the eth-fruit fields and factories, thrown away wiping human Hatchlings' behinds. And the only way to make it stop is to overthrow the Doctors, kill the scheiss-eating Pannas, and let the Klons take over."

Everyone murmured in agreement.

"Hear, hear!" shouted Prospect, climbing up on the table. "Strangle the last Kapo Klon in the entrails of the last Panna!"

"We need to get weapons to our Klons, so they can rise up and kill their masters!"

Rubric felt a chill. She took Salmon Jo's hand. They went outside and sat on the fragrant grass in the dark. "Isn't there some way to have a revolution without violence?" Rubric asked.

"No," Salmon Jo said.

It was nice sometimes how Salmon Jo was so sure of herself. But this was not one of those times.

"I don't like the idea of everyone I've ever known being killed," Rubric said. "Are you okay with that?"

"Of course not," Salmon Jo said. "People who are being killed never like it. I'm just saying, I think they're right. If Society is going to be overthrown, that's probably how it will happen. And I can't blame them. Their point of view is pretty legitimate."

"Well, I can't help them kill all my friends."

"You don't have to."

"But I want to stop slavery. Don't you?"

"It would be nice," Salmon Jo said. "But I don't think I'm cut out for that kind of thing. I hate to be a killjoy, but I'm not sure it's even possible. You're the kind of person who likes to change things. I'm the kind of person who likes to run away."

"We are away," said Rubric, and rested her head on Salmon Jo's shoulder. "And it turns out the only place more awful than Society is here."

"Panna Theodorica said there are other lands," Salmon Jo reminded her. "We could keep traveling."

"What, in our imaginary airship?" Rubric asked. "Good gravy! We can't just leave this hot mess. Can you just imagine Prospect killing all the girls in Yellow Dorm? Filigree Sue hanging by her toes?"

"Don't worry about it," Salmon Jo said. "It's all talk. The Klons have got it good here—they won't go and risk their lives. They just want to get drunk and rant."

Rubric wasn't so sure. "There must be some other way," she said. "If people at home only knew the truth, things would change. What about that documentary we were pretending to make? I could interview the former Klons here, explain what you found in the lab, and pulse the video to people's screens."

"The Doctors would never let anyone see it," Salmon Jo said. "They can monitor the screens. For our health, of course."

"What if I made posters, really well-designed ones with nice graphics, and put them up everywhere. Saying *Klons Are Human*. They wouldn't be able to take them down fast enough."

"I don't know if that phrase would mean anything to people," Salmon Jo said. "It's like saying dogs have five legs. It appears to be not true. And not everyone cares about nice graphics like you do."

Rubric pulled a fistful of grass out of the ground and threw it.

"I hate it here," she said, tearing up. "I just want to go home. But I don't want the Klons to be slaves."

"Look," said Salmon Jo. "I'll find some way to get us out of here. I promise."

CHAPTER TWENTY-TWO

As the fall got colder, Rubric hated the Land of the Barbarous Ones more and more. The more she learned about it, the more she hated it. She and Salmon Jo spent a lot of their time helping Theodorica harvest squash, cook, clean, and do laundry. Theodorica was urging them to take up residence inside the house as the nights became more chilly, but Rubric didn't want to. As long as she and Salmon Jo were sleeping in the tent, it felt like they were only there temporarily.

The structure of a family became clear to Rubric over time, what it meant that Theodorica had a mother, aunt, sister, sister-in-law, niece, and nephew. It seemed that you could never escape your family. They were hung around your neck for life, even if they were annoying and you didn't like them. In Society, you could choose the people you loved, they weren't thrust on you.

Rubric felt especially sorry for Theodorica's little niece, a cute girl named Krizika. She didn't get to grow up in a dorm, surrounded by a hundred playmates eager for games and fellowship. Krizika and her cretinous brother had to share one distracted and overworked mother. There was no team of Nanny Klons whose only job was to care for them. The thing that seemed to take the place of Nanny Klons was the Center for Sons, a collective effort to help women raise the Cretinous Males they were so keen on having. The Center for Sons was the nicest building in the village by far, large and airy, with special gradated lights to help Cretinous Males who were sensitive to changes in illumination.

Salmon Jo was helping out at the Barbarous Ones' lab, just as she had talked about on her first day. The Barbarous Ones were pleased at her willingness to share her knowledge of the process at the Hatchery, and they liked her quick mind. While Salmon Jo was on the cutting edge of Barbarous science, Rubric was doing tasks like shoveling manure. She was never asked to do anything but manual labor. No one appreciated Rubric's art. They had a different aesthetic here—that was the nicest way Rubric could phrase it—and people just grunted at Rubric's attempts to beautify the village. She had given Theodorica a watercolor painting and later found it in the compost pile, neatly shredded for quicker decomposition. The only person who was interested in visual art was Dream, and Rubric spent many long evenings with her in Hot Buttered Toast Town. They egged each other on to greater heights of creativity and self-expression. The low-tech paper the Klons used was a revelation to Rubric, and she loved drawing in charcoal. Rubric spent a lot of time telling Dream about Panna Stencil Pavlina. Dream found the exploits of their Jeepie Similar hilarious. "All she needed was a schatzie," Dream would say. "That's all that matters. I bet if she got a schatzie, she'd start making pretty art again."

The lowest point for Rubric came when Theodorica proudly told her the village had reached a consensus to add a few extra souls to their number because of the excellent harvests they had been having. One of the Jeepie Types—icons—they had chosen was Rubric's.

"I didn't donate any genetic material," Rubric said.

"No, but Dream did."

Rubric was outraged. She didn't want any Jeepie Similar of hers to grow up in this backward place.

"Aren't you afraid the child will grow up to be a worthless artist?" she asked bitterly.

Theodorica laughed. "Your genetics don't determine your destiny. People can be whatever they want."

Salmon Jo wasn't back from the lab in time for dinner that night. Rubric had to eat alone with Theodorica and Branknor again. Rubric decided not to help clean up. Why should she help? She missed Salmon Jo and hated being abandoned with these people.

Rubric sat on the dirt floor in the sitting room, trying to distract herself with a puzzle. A puzzle was another craze of the Barbarous Ones, a tessellation of interlocking pieces that had to be put together in a certain way. The Barbarous Ones had no edfotunement, and Rubric had to do something. Branknor sat near her in an upholstered chair. Rubric no longer feared harmless Branknor. He liked to copy what other people were doing, so he was playing with a puzzle of his own. His was easy, since it came in a sturdy wooden tray with the picture of the puzzle on it, so his only task was to match the few pieces to the picture. A two-year-old girl could put this puzzle together.

Branknor kept interrupting Rubric. "Rooobric, do a puzzle! Yes. Rooobric, do a puzzle with meee!" He'd wave a piece at her until she came over to help him.

The way he said her name was actually kind of cute. He was far from the most horrific Cretinous Male in town. Others were more craggy and hairy than he was. When she'd first laid eyes on him, he seemed ageless. But now she knew he was actually only nineteen. His skin was smoother than older Cretinous Males, and he didn't have a beard, only peach fuzz.

She kept helping him finish the puzzle, but then he would dump the pieces out in his lap and start again. Finally, she abandoned her own puzzle and crouched by the side of his chair. If she gave him the puzzle with just one piece missing, he could slot it in the right place with his pale, slow hands. He could do it if she removed two pieces. But if three were gone, he didn't even try; he just thrust it at her and said, "Do a puzzle, Roooobric!"

"No, no," she said. "You have to do it. I'm tired of doing it for you."

They went back and forth like this for what seemed like forever. Then, finally, Branknor picked up the pieces and began trying to fit them in. He seemed to have no sense that he had to orient the pieces correctly, that the picture on the puzzle should match what was on the wood, or even that the pieces had to go in the holes. But, through trial and error, he was able to slot the pieces in with satisfying clicks. When he had completed it, he laughed and said, "Branknor do a puzzle!" Then he dumped the pieces out again.

Rubric was moderately impressed. She hadn't known he was capable of problem solving. Maybe he wasn't as thicko as she'd thought. This time, she left out four pieces from the completed puzzle. The picture of the puzzle—a poorly drawn dog—began burning itself into her brain.

Salmon Jo came in when Branknor was up to solving five pieces. She got sucked into the puzzle game.

"Fill in the middle and give him the pieces on the edge," she suggested. "Maybe that's easier." She sat down on the arm of the chair. "Move over, Branknor."

Branknor could complete the puzzle with seven pieces missing by the time Theodorica came into the room.

"Look, Branknor can do a puzzle!" Salmon Jo said.

"Look, Branknor can do a puzzle," Branknor affirmed.

"Half a puzzle," Rubric amended.

Theodorica was full of admiration. "He's been messing around with that thing for five years," she said. "You girls are good teachers."

"Pretty soon we'll have him doing the laundry for you," Salmon Jo joked.

Rubric didn't think it was allowed to make fun of how cretinous Branknor was. He was so counterproductive with laundry that it was one of the few tasks Theodorica did without his "help." But Theodorica must have thought it was an okay joke because she laughed like a maniac.

"I could make him a puzzle with fewer pieces," Rubric offered. "One he could do on his own. And I'd make the pieces thicker." Silently she added that she would put a nice picture on the puzzle, not like that cretinous-looking dog.

"That would be very thoughtful," Theodorica said. "Girls, I have some wool overtunics for you. As a gift. It will be so terribly cold in your tent."

In their terribly cold tent, Salmon Jo said, "I'm learning more about those boluses of medicine the Sons take. At first, I was so cynical after everything we've been through that I wondered if the medicine even helped, or if it only made the Sons worse, or if they might even be making their Sons more cretinous on purpose. But it's all completely aboveboard, and it's actually a really promising treatment. They're taking these quaternary ammonium cations that have been biosynthesized from amino—"

"C'mon, Salmon Jo," Rubric grumbled. She knew pretending to listen to Salmon Jo's scientific rambling was part of being a good schatzie, but she was too miserable.

"Okay, sorry. How about this? I think the Sons are really fun."

"They don't bother me anymore," Rubric admitted. "I don't know about fun."

"I really get it now, why they like having the Sons around the place. They're very pure people. What you see is what you get. And even though they're cretinous, they're good at some things, but it's unpredictable and they need a lot of coaching. I think Branknor understands more than he can express. He always knows how Theodorica is feeling, and she's hard to read. All the emotional stuff is there."

Salmon Jo seemed to be paying plenty of attention to the Cretinous Males and their emotions. Then why couldn't she see how lonely and sad Rubric was?

"The Barbarous Ones have just bought into a mass delusion that Cretinous Males are really glam, just like we have our mass delusion about the Klons," Rubric said.

"Maybe every place has their own delusion. But I think the one here is better, kinder. You know how before we left home I said I didn't know what human was? I know now. The Sons taught me what it means to be a human being. Even if they're sick or not brainy, they're just as human as us. I think they make you learn more about yourself, and that's why the Barbarous Ones think they're such an asset."

"You're fitting right in here," Rubric said acidly. "I bet you like the pregnancy thing too."

"The pregnancy thing is interesting," Salmon Jo said, ignoring Rubric's tone. "It's kind of amazing that the human body can naturally do all those things that are so hard to replicate in the Hatchery. Theodorica says giving birth is like going through the fence. It hurts, but afterward, you don't remember the pain very well. But childbirth doesn't cause seizures, and at the end of it you get a Hatchling."

"Would you...you would never do that, would you?"

"I wouldn't rule it out as completely out of the question, someday," Salmon Jo said.

Rubric buried her head in her hands.

"I mean, if my schatzie wasn't against it, which I'm assuming you would be, based on what you're doing right now, if you were my schatzie..." Salmon Jo trailed off.

At this moment, the chances of being Salmon Jo's schatzie in future years seemed low.

"But we're going back," Rubric reminded her. "Right?"

"Right."

"When?"

Salmon Jo sighed. "I don't know. I'm really scared of the fence. Of dying. Don't tell Dream, but she didn't do me any favors, grabbing my hand when we crossed the fence. I think that made us into kind of a circuit, and the current flowed through us more."

"Really? You never told me that. Maybe when you go back, then, everything will be fine!"

"Yeah, maybe. Or maybe not. It's not the kind of gamble I like to take with my life. I'm working on another way to cross the fence. I've got a project going. But it might take a while."

"A while?" Rubric rolled her eyes, and then realized Salmon Jo couldn't see her in the dark. "What does that even mean?"

"I don't know!" shouted Salmon Jo. "Why are you being so mean?"

"Because you're just pretending that we're going back someday," Rubric said. "You like it here. And we'll just stay here longer and longer. And then someday you'll say, oh, my project didn't work out, sorry."

Rubric heard Salmon Jo swallowing loudly, a sure sign she was crying, or about to.

"What else is it that you want me to do? I do like it here. And I don't know what there is for us at home except getting captured and treatment. We were incredibly lucky. But the Doctors won't stay bumblingly incompetent forever, if we keep stealing all their Klons and trying to topple Society. It's safer for us here. The only thing that motivates me to want to go back is you." Her voice cracked, and now she was crying. "I thought you were getting to like it here."

"Aha, so you admit it! You're trying to stall me here forever."

"No," said Salmon Jo. "Well, maybe, in a way. You're getting used to the Sons, you're fond of Branknor, you're going to make him puzzles. I thought maybe you found something that was meaningful for you."

"Good gravy! Just because I don't hate Branknor doesn't mean I want to live out my days surrounded by Cretinous Males. And making puzzles? You really think I can find meaning in my life making toys for drooling Sons when the Klons are still enslaved? I am miserable here!"

"It's not like you've even tried to fit in," Salmon Jo said. "Have you thought about me for one second? I've dreamed all my life about studying the Sons. This is my big opportunity, and

you're all '*Waah, waah,* I don't like picking apples. Let's go.'
You just have a bad attitude."

Rubric was infuriated. "I don't have to have a good attitude.
I can't believe I fell for your lies. 'Don't worry, Rubric, we're
leaving, I promise.' You know what? If you like the Cretinous
Males so much, live with them forever! Give birth to one! What
do I care? I don't need a schatzie who lies to me, and tries to
manipulate me, and doesn't care how I feel. Get out, go sleep in
the house. Go sleep with Theodorica. Go sleep with Branknor!"

Salmon Jo unzipped the tent and left without a word. Alone
in the tent, Rubric cried herself to sleep. She shivered all night,
from cold and from sadness.

The next morning, Dream came to visit Rubric. She told her
she was going back home to free more Klons.

"People are too complacent," Dream said. "They like to talk
about rebellion while sitting in their rocking chairs by the fire.
It's nice here, but I can't sit around doing sweet scheiss nothing.
Prospect doesn't want to go. But I told her I won't be gone long.
It'll just be a quick trip, in and out. Help some Klons out, and be
back before she knows it. A little raid. You want to come?"

"Yes," Rubric said. "I'm like you. I can't stand by while this
is going on. Someone's got to do something."

And that was the way Rubric sold it to Salmon Jo. Her
burning desire to help others and end slavery. It was hard for
Salmon Jo to argue with such lofty motives. But Rubric didn't
even believe herself. If she looked inside her heart, was she really
that noble? Maybe she just had a burning desire to get out of the
Land of the Barbarous Ones, and never come back.

CHAPTER TWENTY-THREE

It was just dawn, and everything was bathed in an unreal
light. As much as Rubric hated the fence and the Land of
the Barbarous Ones, she had to admit the desert surrounding the
fence was beautiful. The black silhouette of the wall beyond the
fence was melting into reds and yellows as the sunlight touched
it.

"I'll be back so soon," Rubric promised for the millionth
time. "Don't worry."

Salmon Jo didn't say anything. They had said everything,
over and over again. They held each other tightly, kissing tenderly,
deeply. Rubric threaded her fingers through Salmon Jo's coarse
hair, caressing her head. She wanted this good-bye kiss to be
enough, but it could never be enough. How could saying good-
bye to Salmon Jo ever feel complete and acceptable?

Rubric and Salmon Jo had formally made up after their fight.
But there was still a wedge between them. It was the only thing
that made it possible for Rubric to leave her. Maybe if Salmon Jo
had objected more strenuously, Rubric would have stayed. But
Salmon Jo had accepted her decision meekly.

"I'm sorry I couldn't build that rubber suit to cross the fence
in," Salmon Jo said finally.

"It's okay," Rubric said, stroking her earlobe. "You shouldn't
come. I don't want you to have a seizure and die."

Nearby, Dream and Prospect were embracing and murmuring their own farewells.

She couldn't tell Salmon Jo this, but Rubric was looking forward to having adventures. She was proud of being one of the only ones willing to actually do anything about Society. And, of course, she was delighted to leave the Land of the Barbarous Ones.

"I could camp here and wait for you," Salmon Jo suggested.

"Don't do that," Rubric said. "We could cross the fence anywhere. It might not be at Lvodz."

Saying the last good-bye was the hardest part. Rubric kissed her favorite spot on Salmon Jo's neck.

The next hardest part was running through the fence. Knowing what it would be like didn't help much. Once again, every muscle, sinew, and bone in her body quivered in pain as she ran through the invisible fence. Her blood felt like it was sizzling, and her heart stuttered.

The third hardest part was the wall. This time, they had grappling hooks and a real rope ladder. But there was no Salmon Jo to help. It took them a long time to get over the wall. On the top of the wall, Rubric stood and waved both arms to Salmon Jo. Then Rubric felt light-headed, so she quickly jumped down.

The electric bikes were waiting right where they'd left them. The battery case had cracked on one, so they shared the other. They had planned this trip as carefully as they could, and their Klon-freeing mission had three parts. The first stop was just outside Iron City at a factory that processed eth fruits into ethanol. The Klon they planned to free was Salmon Jo's Jeepie Similar, just as they had freed Dream, who was Rubric's Jeepie Similar. It helped Rubric to justify the trip to herself.

The whole ride to Iron City, Rubric had a ringing in her ears from going through the fence. Mercifully, it had stopped by the time they reached the bike parking lot of the ethanol factory. They wheeled the bike over to a charging station and plugged it in.

"What does this Klon do here again?" Rubric asked. She was feeling confident. It felt good to be back in Society, even as a fugitive.

"She cleans up the waste product that the factory generates," Dream said. "Shoveling sludge into bins."

"It makes no sense that they would give someone of Salmon Jo's Jeepie Type that assignment," Rubric said, smacking down the sticky kickstand on the e-bike. "Anyone can do that job. Why would you utilize someone with so much brains for that?"

Dream shook her head. "You still don't understand how it is. They don't want to use a Klon's brain. The smarter they are, the more likely they'll be stuck off doing something soul-crushing and menial." She smiled. "C'mon, let's go. I'm ready to impersonate a Panna."

The factory's front office was incredibly busy, Klons racing back and forth waving screens and shouting. But, of course, they made time for a couple of Pannas. Rubric and Dream played cute with the Kapo Klon.

"We're doing a report on eth fruits for academy!" Dream said, tilting her head to the side in a fetching way. To Rubric's critical eye, Dream was overdoing her imitation of a pampered, mindless human. But the Klon seemed besotted.

"We're following eth fruits from their earliest days on the tree until they are turned into energy!" Rubric said, giggling.

"Charming," declared the Kapo Klon, an older woman with a lined face. "I will personally escort you around the factory."

"That's not necessary," Dream said.

"Oh, but it is," the Kapo Klon said. "There are a lot of dangers in a factory for young Pannas like yourselves."

Dream's smile began to look a little strained. But Rubric knew a Panna could always get her own way. "We must go by ourselves," she said haughtily. "It's part of the assignment."

"In that case," demurred the Kapo Klon.

Rubric was actually a little shocked at how easy it was. Security was so lax in Society. They could probably do a lot more damage to this factory than just steal one Klon.

"Are you thinking what I'm thinking?" Rubric asked, as they walked through a dirty hallway, clutching floor plans and safety equipment.

"I know you're thinking we could destroy this factory while we're here, and I agree," Dream said. "But that's not what I'm thinking."

"Okay, what are you thinking?"

"I'm thinking it's so much fun to be a Panna!" said Dream.

They found the staircase that led down to the basement where Salmon Jo's Jeepie Similar Klon was working. They donned the face masks and polycarbonate goggles that the Kapo Klon had told them to wear.

When they reached the basement, they couldn't see at all. The whole area was a cloud of white dust. They could hear Klons talking and coughing, but they couldn't see them. Rubric turned on the flashlight she kept in her pocket, but it only made the cloud of dust more luminescent. They walked around, peering at each Klon they saw. Big chutes came down from the ceiling, emptying piles of eth-fruit detritus into dumpsters, but the white dust settled all over the room. The Klons were scraping the white stuff into piles and then shoveling the piles into the dumpsters. Finally, Rubric caught sight of a characteristic stooped posture at the other end of the large room. Even through the white swirl, she recognized Salmon Jo's Jeepie Similar Klon.

The girl was younger than Rubric, barely into her teens, but she was gaunt and hunched. Her face was covered in white dust. Her golden eyes seemed to pop out of her goggles.

"Hello," Dream said, and the girl jumped.

"Are you inspectors?" she said. "I'm sorry I'm not wearing my mask. Kapo Klon always tells me to put it on."

They had agreed that Dream had to handle the big reveal. "No offense, Panna Rubric, but you did a lousy job," Dream had said. "You seemed completely veruckt. Leave it to me. And be ready to run, because some Klons are very loyal and aren't receptive to the idea of escape. I know that seems strange, but that is how it is."

Now, Dream knocked the girl on the arm. "Listen, Gold Eyes, I know your Kapo Klon doesn't want you to wear a mask.

'Cause it makes you breathe too slow, and then you work too slow, eh? You know how I know?" Dream was using what sounded to Rubric like an exaggerated Klon accent.

The girl's eyes got wider and she shook her head.

"Eh, I'm a Klon too," Dream whispered.

"You're her personal Klon?"

"Keep your voice down! No, I was a Picker Klon. Maybe I picked some of the eth fruits you're shoveling now. But I escaped. This Panna human helped me. If you want, we can take you to the Land of the Barbarous Ones."

The girl began to tremble. The trembling started her coughing.

"The Land of the Barbarous Ones isn't as good or as bad as the stories say," Dream whispered. "They really do have Cretinous Males and give birth to Hatchlings out of their you-know-whats. They're odd people, but they leave you alone. Know why? Because you're free there, a Panna, a human. You still have to work, but only half as much, and it's real gentle work. So what do you say, Gold Eyes, are you coming or what?"

The girl tried to answer, but she was racked by coughing. "Do I have to decide right now?" she choked out.

Rubric felt so sorry for her. "No, of c—"

Dream slapped Rubric's arm, silencing her. "Yes, Klon, it's now or never. This is your once-in-a-lifetime chance. But we're not trying to sell you anything. We've got a list of suitable Klons as long as your arm, and if you don't want to go, we just move on to the next. Only don't tell anyone what we said, or we'll come back and smother you in your sleep. From the sound of your lungs, it wouldn't take very long."

"It's difficult to make such a hasty decision," she said. "I need more…" She sighed. She looked like she might just fall asleep on her feet.

"Data?" Rubric suggested. Salmon Jo was always saying she needed more data before she could decide anything.

The girl just looked blankly at her. Where was this girl's lightning-fast intelligence? From what Rubric could see through the dust cloud around her, other figures were shuffling closer. They probably wanted to hear what they were saying. Dream needed to wrap this up.

"Why am I on the list?"

"The Panna here's got a soft spot for your Jeepie Type," Dream said. "Her snuggle mate is the same Jeepie Type."

Now the girl looked alarmed.

"It's not like that," Rubric assured her. "I only have eyes for my schatzie. She's back in the Land of the Barbarous Ones. Also, your Jeepie Type is very brainy. We need people like that."

The girl smiled faintly. "No one's ever called me brainy before."

"All right, brainy, we're leaving. Are you coming?" Dream asked.

"Yes," she said, in the most indecisive way you could possibly say yes.

"What's something that breaks down in this factory that we might need your help with fixing?" Rubric asked.

"The cane-splash mixer is always getting sucrolated," the Klon replied.

They shuffled through the sugar mist toward the elevator they had spotted earlier.

"The cave splasher is sugarcoated," Dream announced to no one in particular.

"She means the cane-splash mixer is sucrolated," Rubric said louder, smacking Dream.

"Not again," someone said.

"I can help," said another.

"Nah, we got it covered," Dream said.

In the elevator, they removed their goggles and safety masks. Dream shook out her tunic and brushed at her leggings, but Rubric didn't bother.

"The floor plan said the back door is on the ground level," Dream said.

"Yeah, but the finished ethanol is on the mezzanine level," Rubric said.

The girl just followed them without comment, although she was a bit startled when Rubric stopped in the hallway and smashed the glass on the fire-alarm panel with her flashlight. She pulled the fire-alarm handle, and a loud bell began ringing.

"So do they even let you guys out of the building if there's a fire?" Dream asked. "Or do you have to keep working?"

"They let us out," the girl said. "They removed some fire-alarm panels because we set off a lot of false alarms so we could have breaks. But we have drills all the time. If we all got toasted up, they'd have to get all new Klons who wouldn't know how to do things. Our jobs are harder than they look."

"Looks hard enough already," Dream said. "What do you work, twelve-hour days?"

"Sixteen, sometimes," the Klon said. "Without our long hours, Society would grind to a halt." Talking about numbers seemed to soothe her. Rubric wondered if Dream had noticed and that was why she had asked.

"How many minutes does it take everyone in the factory to exit during a fire drill?" Rubric asked. Dream smiled at her, but there was a reason Rubric wanted to know.

"Just four minutes," the Klon answered. Rubric knew she could trust her response.

Rubric checked the watch around her neck. It had been Salmon Jo's, and she had given it to Rubric. "It's probably safe to start a fire now," she said.

"How can it be safe to start a fire?" the girl asked.

Rubric pushed open the door that led to the finished ethanol storeroom. Another alarm went off, but it didn't matter. The big room had many fans turning lazily on the ceiling and was filled one end to the other with tanks of ethanol. There were several fire extinguishers placed on the walls next to the doors. Rubric took two and tossed them to the Klon and Dream. The Klon dropped hers on the floor, and some foam hissed out. Rubric went to work with her pocket knife, poking a tiny hole in the sealed spigot of the nearest tank.

"Um," said the Klon. "I don't know if this is such—"

Rubric took her flint out of her pocket and struck it. A spark appeared, and she was able to light her cloth safety mask. The girl edged closer to the door, speechless.

Rubric stuck the flaming mask in the spigot of the tank. Nothing happened, and she was thinking it wasn't going to work when *whumph!* a huge flame shot up. She turned and ran.

Rubric heard a successive series of *whumph*s behind her as the other tanks began to catch. She bumped into the Klon, who dropped her fire extinguisher again. Dream and Rubric were running for the stairs, trying to drag the girl with them.

"No, close the door, close the door!" cried the girl, bumping into Rubric in her frenzy to get back, past them, the other way to shut the door. She slammed the metal door shut just as balls of flame belched out of the doorway. When she turned back again, she had no eyebrows. But Rubric had no time to look. The three of them kept jostling each other on the stairs in a way that would have been comical if it wasn't so scary. She did notice with part of her brain that the girl wasn't racing far ahead of them as she would have expected. Maybe if your lungs were full of dust, you wouldn't be in top running condition like Salmon Jo.

They burst out the door, through the parking lot, and into the underbrush.

"The bike is no good for three people," Rubric said.

Dream cradled her head in her hands. "What kind of thicko am I? Why are we only thinking of that now?"

Rubric went to get the bike anyway. She didn't know what else to do.

They crept through the scrub to the car parking lot on the other side of the factory, Rubric pushing the e-bike. The trees were thin, and they could have been seen easily if anyone had looked in their direction. But no one was. Although the parking lot was jammed with every Factory Klon, they were all gazing up at the building.

It was a magnificent fire. Rubric was surprised it had spread so quickly. Walls of red fire shot up everywhere, and the brick building was blackening. Every now and then, there would be a small explosion from within. The roof was warping and buckling. Glass windows burst outward.

In the parking lot, Kapo Klons began taking attendance. Then a fire truck pulled up, sirens wailing. Firefighters, Klons in green uniforms and Pannas in dirty white ones, leapt out of the truck and began uncoiling a long hose. Rubric was watching with interest when Dream grabbed her arm and pointed to something.

A van. The key was in the ignition. Nearby, a Repair Klon and her human manager were standing around, gawking like everyone else. They had probably arrived in the van right before the fire started.

"Do you know how to drive?" she asked Dream.

"No. Do you?"

"No."

The Klon was shaking her head.

"I've played a lot of VR driving games," Rubric said.

"Well, great! How hard can it be?" asked Dream.

They walked nonchalantly over to the van. Rubric could see there were only two seats.

"You climb in the back," Rubric told the golden-eyed girl and brought the e-bike around to the rear of the van with her. Was the back unlocked? Yes. The girl silently helped Rubric lift the bike inside and then climbed inside herself, wedging herself among tools, hardware, cans of paint, and the bike. She swung the doors in but didn't close them all the way. Probably afraid it would be too loud. The van's rightful owners were still standing around, looking at the blazing building.

Rubric hopped into the driver's seat and Dream into the passenger seat. Quick as she could, she turned the key. The engine started up, but so did a horrible dinging sound. The repair people turned around.

"Hurry, hurry, hurry!" Dream shouted unhelpfully. Rubric accidentally hit something that made the windshield wipers turn on. She tried to move the gear stick to a different position, but it wouldn't move.

There was a woman running up to the car. Without hardly looking up, Rubric swung the door open and hit her with it. Oh, in the VR games you had to step on the brake! She found the brake and was able to move the gear stick. She stepped on the gas and the car zoomed backwards.

"Wrong way, wrong way!" Dream shouted. Again, unhelpfully.

It took Rubric a little while to find the brake again, but a tree stopped them, anyway. While she was trying to figure out the gear stick, a woman ran up to the passenger side and opened the door, grabbing Dream. She shrieked.

Rubric stepped on the gas again, and they lurched forward. The woman holding Dream fell, and Dream slammed the door shut again.

Rubric made a very wide turn out of the parking lot. They began careening down the road.

"Can't you go any faster?" Dream asked.

Rubric sped up. She accidentally clipped a couple of mirrors off parked cars. "Oops."

"There's a Security vehicle behind us," Dream shouted, looking into her own side mirror. "Do something!"

"Like what?"

"Oh wow!" Dream said. She rolled down her window and stuck her head out to get a better look. She was almost decapitated when Rubric risked a look in her own mirror and swerved all over the road. Every time Rubric moved her eyes, her stiff, terrified arms gripping the steering wheel followed.

"Gold Eyes is throwing stuff out the back," Dream reported. "Good gravy! She just threw a can of paint, and it smashed into their windscreen. They're slowing down."

But Rubric had to slow down too to go around a corner.

"Quick, turn here," Dream said. "While they can't see you."

"Here?"

"No, not into the bush! Where the road is."

Their new road was straight and empty. Rubric pressed the gas pedal all the way to the floor.

After a while Dream said, "There's no one back there. Maybe you should pull into one of these driveways. Woah, slow down!"

The van was nicely hidden, half behind a hedge and half in the hedge. Rubric turned the key. "Wait, was I supposed to put it in park before I turned it off?"

They spilled out of the van and ran around the back to check on Gold Eyes. She was unharmed and glowed at their praise of her quick thinking. A minute later, they saw the Security vehicle fly by. Dream thought they should get back on the road right away, but Rubric's hands were shaking too bad to drive. To calm down, she started questioning the girl about her life.

Her garbled account suggested she had been working in the factory since she was nine. They had need of small nimble hands. She had fond memories of the Klon academy, where she had grown up until then. Dream was able to draw her out to a certain extent by talking about Klon academy games and customs.

Then Rubric got the idea to paint the van so it would be hard to recognize. Forty minutes later, the van was bright orange and said *R.D. Construction, since 2379* in Rubric's neat lettering.

CHAPTER TWENTY-FOUR

Rubric wanted to rest some more, but Dream insisted they move on to their second task immediately. "We have to hit them *boom, boom, boom*," she said. "Once they realize we do stuff like this, it's going to get a lot harder. Plus, I told Prospect it would take no time."

"Of course," said Rubric, getting up quickly. She thought of her last glimpse of Salmon Jo, waving on the other side of the fence.

It was two hours' ride to Velvet City, and they arrived at dusk to Dream's old eth-fruit farm. They knew they would both be recognized there, and they knew there was no way Gold Eyes could pass for a Panna. Rubric couldn't even identify the quality she had that made her Klon-like. But she had it and she couldn't pass. So they sent her in posing as a Delivery Klon, and while she was there, she passed the word to the Picker Klons that there was going to be a big fire in forty-five minutes. Instead of going to the rehearsed fire drill location, they should all go to the tree closest to the front gate and get in the van.

This fire was harder to light, and less spectacular. But the smoke smelled better, almost sweet, as the eth-fruit trees caught alight. The flames crackled against the black sky.

"Do you think our Jeepie Type is a pyromaniac?" she asked Dream.

"Some kind of maniac," she agreed.

It was chaotic as the Klons showed up at the van, some dragging pillowcases full of possessions. They all piled into the back.

"There are supposed to be twice as many as this," Rubric said.

"Scheiss, I hope we haven't burnt them up," Dream fretted.

"We need to go before the fire trucks get here," Rubric told her.

"Let's wait a little longer," Dream said. "I think more are coming."

But Rubric heard the sirens. "We go now," she said, and started the engine. Dream sucker punched her. Rubric saw stars, just like animated characters did on edfotunement.

"No, no, we're leaving," Rubric said through the stars, and the van lurched forward. Screams from the back, as Klons fell over. She heard someone shut the door. Good, very good. She took off as fast as she dared down the bumpy road, heading northeast, back toward the Land of the Barbarous Ones.

They pulled over about ten minutes later so the Klons could cut out their chips. Even with their well-stocked first aid kit and sterilized scalpels, the leafy ground looked like an abattoir within two minutes. Rubric couldn't stand it and thought she might throw up, so she climbed back into the driver's seat of the van. First she left the door open, but she could still hear the Klons' gasps of pain. She chunked the door closed and rolled up the windows. As keyed up as she was, she was even more tired, and she was almost asleep when Dream got into the van.

"We're ready to set out," she said. She had blood on her tunic. "Onward!"

"I just couldn't help," Rubric said. "I just couldn't."

"That's okay," Dream said. "You Pannas are a bunch of softies. I'm sorry I hit you. But I think Klons were still coming when we left. I feel bad about leaving them behind. I wonder if they're going to get in trouble."

"I made the decision that it was time to go," Rubric said. "Someone had to do it."

"Yeah," Dream said. She let out a quavering sigh.

"Do you think we should paint the van again?" they both said in unison.

Sometimes Rubric felt like she *was* Dream.

They decided the darkness of the night would be their best disguise, so they set off. The driving was easier when Dream discovered a mechanism to turn on the van's headlamps. Rubric could go a lot faster now. They arrived at the wall around three a.m.

"I can't believe I just crossed the fence less than twenty-four hours ago," Dream said. "This has been the longest day of my life."

"I hope the Klons will be okay crossing the fence," Rubric said.

"Poor little piglets," said Dream.

When they opened the back of the van, for a second Rubric was afraid all the Klons were dead. They were all sprawled on the floor in a big heap. But they began lifting their heads and blinking.

"Wake up, my companions!" Dream said. "It's time to cross the fence to your new life." One by one, the women and girls hopped out of the van.

"Here's flashlights, a grappling hook, and a rope ladder," Dream said. "Empty your pockets of metal before you cross the fence, and don't hold hands. It hurts like you wouldn't believe. If anyone falls down and starts twitching, just make sure they don't hurt themselves, and don't put nothing in their mouths. Roll them on their sides when they're done having a fit, and wait for them to feel better. Here's a map to get you to Hot Buttered Toast Town. By the way, there aren't actually any vodka waterfalls—I know that's disappointing. Take care of Gold Eyes here. If you run into any bad trouble, our friend Salmon Jo made these flares you can light, and she'll come get you. But she made them herself and she's a bit of a nut, so who knows? It might blow up in your face or something, so be careful. We're crossing tomorrow ourselves if all goes well. Is that all clear?"

Rubric could barely follow all the information Dream had just spewed out, and she knew it all already. There was no way these Klons could have taken all that in. But they just nodded and began gathering their belongings.

"Clear as mud," said one older woman. "Let's go! See you on the other side."

"Tomorrow," Dream agreed.

Rubric watched them leave, but they were invisible almost instantly. Little bright spots from their flashlights bobbed in the dark like fireflies. After a while, she started hearing clanks and thumps.

"They're climbing over the wall," she whispered. She didn't know why she was whispering.

"Good gravy, imagine doing that in the dark," Dream said in her normal voice. "I bet they wish they'd stayed at the farm."

Soon there were no more thuds, and all was silent.

"Are they over?" Rubric asked.

"How should I know?" Dream said. "Let's go. There's sweet scheiss nothing we can do for them now."

As they returned to the van, Rubric wondered how they had become brutal adventurers so quickly. She had been motivated by her desire to help these people and by her squishy feelings about how much she loved justice and fairness and humanity. But while they were doing the operation, as she now thought of it, the Klons became just so many logistical problems, and she had no squishy feelings at all. Bundle them into the van, bundle them over the wall. Maybe later on, when she got back to the Land of the Barbarous Ones, they could all get together and sing songs and share their thoughts and emotions.

They started driving, toward Lvodz. Rubric thought she was getting good at this driving thing, except her eyes kept closing for half a second.

"Talk to me," she ordered. "Sing, whatever."

"Um, what do those dials and lights on the dashboard mean?" Dream wanted to know.

"I have no idea! And if I take my eyes off the road to look at them, we may swerve right off."

"It's just that two red lights are flashing."

"Not good."

Soon they came to a red stoplight. There was no one around, so Rubric wasn't sure if she had to stop, but she figured it was better to obey the guidelines of the road when you were a serial arsonist fugitive. While she was stopped, she dared to glance at the dashboard, but she couldn't interpret the flashing lights, either.

"Hmm. There's a screen with instructions in that mitten department thing. You could look at that," she suggested to Dream.

"In the *what*?"

"I'm not sure what it's called, okay? It's that little hatch right in front of you."

Dream fumbled around and found it. She pulled out a screen, which was attached to the inside of the hatch by a cable. "I've never really used a screen before," she said. "And I'm not much of a reader. Oh good, there's lots of graphics."

While Dream was consulting the screen, Rubric pulled over for a nap. She woke up feeling refreshed, but when she tried to start the van nothing happened.

"Oh," said Dream. "I was afraid of that. If I'm understanding this right, we've run out of electricity. We need to plug in somewhere."

They both looked around at the desolate landscape. There were woods. There was the road. Off in the distance, Rubric could see a stream.

"But it was sunny all day, and there are panels on the roof," Rubric protested.

"Send a pulse to whoever designed the van and complain to them," Dream said. "There's sweet scheiss nothing I can do about it."

"It looks like it's back to the electric bike for us," groaned Rubric. "And we're still fifteen klicks from Lvodz."

"Let's get some more sleep first," Dream suggested. "I can barely think. This is a pretty isolated area. I want to go into those scraggly woods there, where we can keep the van in sight."

Rubric would have preferred to stay in the van. The driver's seat was surprisingly comfy. But Dream insisted that they not only go to the woods but bring the e-bike and all their stuff.

In the end, Rubric was glad they had. They slept later than they had planned to, and soon after they awoke, a security vehicle pulled up beside the van. A bunch of people swarmed out. From their hiding place, the girls couldn't tell if they were Klons, Pannas, or both, and they couldn't quite hear what they said. But they practically tore the van apart. They were still there when Rubric and Dream dragged the bike through the woods so they could emerge on another road.

Even though Lvodz was such a small city, they found a Comfort Station. It made Rubric think of the night she and Salmon Jo had gone to the Comfort Station at home in Mountain City and eaten tea and toast, the same night they had broken into the Hatchery. It seemed like a lifetime ago. Rubric forced herself to think about the present. She wasn't there for reminiscing or even resting. Rubric had to use the bathroom to change and freshen up. For the last leg of their operation, she had to again look like a clean, glam Panna, not a stinky, smoke-blackened Klon. In fact, this time, she had to look like a Doctor.

Rubric and Dream had chosen the final Klon to free because she was another of their Jeepie Similars, and it was such a nice coincidence to find one in Lvodz, the closest city to where they had crossed the fence both times. Rubric felt almost relaxed after having slept, washed her face, and put on clean clothes. This should be the easiest of the three Klon-freeing adventures, since she didn't plan to set any fires. It was just a simple impersonation.

Theodorica was a great hand with a needle. From Rubric's sketches, she had created a wonderful replica of a Doctor's saffron robe. She'd had to sew weights into the hem to make it fall just right. The Klons in the Comfort Station lowered their heads respectfully when Rubric emerged, ostensibly a Doctor.

According to the information she had, the Jeepie Similar Klon was just Rubric's age, with a nice assignment as a lifeguard at the city pool. Rubric walked to the pool, only about half a klick away, while Dream rode the e-bike. Rubric couldn't picture a Doctor riding an e-bike and thought it would look suspicious. When she arrived at the pool's entrance, she saw Dream waiting with the bike. But she didn't acknowledge her. Rubric swept magisterially through the building to the poolside. No one questioned her. Girls screamed and splashed in the saltwater pool, while Pannas swam laps in one roped-off lane.

The Lifeguard Klon sat on a tall white chair by the deep end. Rubric didn't think she could ever get used to seeing her Jeepie Similars. This girl looked more like her, even, than Dream. The only distinction that Rubric could make was this girl had a mole on her right cheek. And freckles, probably from being in the sun all the time. She wore her hair a bit longer and had bangs.

The girl had been lifting her whistle to her lips, but she let it drop when she saw Doctor Rubric. Rubric had never seen such horror on anyone's face.

"Not me," she whispered. "I've been so good."

"Come with me," Rubric said sternly.

"I'm not allowed to leave my post," she said. "The girls might drown."

"Another Klon is coming to take your place," Rubric lied.

The girl's eyes flicked around, as if she was searching for the backup security a real Doctor would have. But she slid off her lifeguard's chair and followed Rubric. There was a moment where Rubric was afraid she would push her into the pool and pull a runner, but she didn't.

The original plan had been to get the girl onto the electric bike, get her out of here, and then explain everything. They had lost a lot of time trying to explain things to Gold Eyes. But on the spur of the moment, Rubric decided to change the plan. This girl was so skittish. It was hard to imagine herself in the girl's position, but Rubric didn't think she would get on a bike with some menacing Doctor. So Rubric led the girl into the locker room.

There were at least a dozen women by the lockers. That was inconvenient. Rubric brought the girl to the communal shower area, where there was just one Panna showering. Rubric envied her. Showers were unknown in the Land of the Barbarous Ones, and their bathwater was never hot enough.

"Get out," Rubric told the Panna showering. And she did, even though she was covered in soap! She didn't even stop to turn the water off. This Doctor's robe was magic.

"I'm not really a Doctor," she told the girl. The girl's eyes flitted again, as if this time she was looking for cameras. "And this is not for edfotunement, either. I'm part of a secret organization that thinks it's wrong that Klons have to do all the work." That sounded good, didn't it? "I'm here to take you to the Land of the Barbarous Ones, where Klons are free." She hated doing all this promotion for the Land of the Barbarous Ones, but Dream had been adamant that this was the simplest way to explain.

The water from the shower sputtered and hissed as Rubric and her Jeepie Similar stared at each other.

"You're not a Doctor," the girl reviewed. "You're not taking me for treatment."

"Right," Rubric affirmed.

"Give me your robe," the girl said.

"What? Why?"

"I need to know I can trust you," the girl said. "I'm sure you have your own angle, just like everyone else in the world."

"Fine," said Rubric, and she took off her robe.

The girl shook it out and tried it on.

"Do I look like a Doctor?" she asked, pivoting.

"Very much so."

The girl smiled. "I still don't trust you," she said. Then she punched Rubric in the stomach.

Rubric doubled over, staggered, and slipped on the wet floor. It happened so fast, but her mind seemed to be working slowly. *Why do my Jeepie Similars keep hitting me?* she wondered. *I've never hit anyone!*

As if in slow motion, she saw the girl grab a bottle of chlorine and uncap it. Then Rubric screamed in pain as the scalding liquid splashed onto her.

By the time she stopped screaming, the girl was long gone, but a crowd of people had gathered.

Some people seemed to think she was the Lifeguard Klon, even though she wasn't wearing a bathing suit. These people scolded her. Others seemed to think she was a Panna. One woman helped her get under a cold shower. The cold felt good, but the spray of the water on her skin was too hard. Although she was soaking wet, her skin felt like it was on fire.

A Security Klon pushed her way to the front. Belatedly, Rubric realized that she should have made herself scarce.

"What happened here?" the Klon demanded. Rubric noticed she didn't call her Panna.

"I am a Doctor," Rubric said. She tried to speak in a dignified way between gasps of pain. "I was here to take a Klon for treatment. But she attacked me."

"There was a Doctor here," one Panna murmured. "Is that her?"

"Uh-huh," said the Security Klon. "So, Doctor, where's your security team? Where's your robe?"

"She stole my robe," Rubric said.

"And how did she come to do that? Can I see your identity card?"

"She took that too."

"What's your name, Doctor? Where do you work?"

They had rehearsed this, but everything had fallen out of Rubric's head. "Uh," she said. She had to say a name quickly, or they would know she was lying. "I'm Panna Theodorica." It was the first name that came into her head. "I mean Doctor Theodorica." Theodorica was a Barbarous name. It wasn't a noun, like a name should be. Totally unbelievable. "I don't have time to talk to you. Let me through!"

She tried to make a run for it, but the ring of people tightened around her. They wouldn't let her out. Good citizens all, they grabbed her burned arms and restrained her.

"I saw her give the robe to the other one," someone said. "I think they're in cahoots."

"But the other one hit her. I saw it!"

"She's clearly a Panna. Maybe she's gone veruckt."

The Security Klon tied her hands behind her back with a plastic wire specially designed for the purpose, apologizing all the while. The plastic cuffs dug into her burned wrists.

The Klon pulsed the hospital. Rubric's heart sank when she heard her say, "I'm not sure, Doctor, but I think she's the Jeepie Type we got the special pulse about."

Rubric didn't resist when she was loaded into the ambulance. Two Medical Assistant Klons spread some kind of green goop on her skin that made it feel better. There were oval windows in the back of the ambulance. Rubric thought she saw Dream out on the street, looking worried, but she might have imagined that.

CHAPTER TWENTY-FIVE

It took the Doctors no time to identify Rubric. They had suspected who she was from the start, and then they rolled her fingertips on a handheld scanner.

"That's her fingerprints all right," confirmed the Doctor.

Every year during her annual physical exam, they had done that procedure. Rubric had always naively assumed it had something to do with her health. But she saw now that it was their way of preventing switching and impersonation, since everyone, even people of the same Jeepie Type, had unique fingerprints.

The Doctor who dealt with Rubric's case looked so much like her old friend Filigree Sue that Rubric thought she must be her Jeepie Similar. But she acted nothing like her. This Doctor was smarter and meaner. Maybe she wasn't the same Jeepie Type. Rubric considered the issue as a Medical Assistant Klon treated her burns, and the Doctor relentlessly questioned her. The Klon's touch was as gentle as the Doctor's tone was harsh.

"Did you steal a Klon from Sweet Fruit Farm near Velvet City?

"Did you set fire to Blue River Ethanol Factory in Iron City and steal a Klon?

"Did you not only steal more Klons but actually burn Sweet Fruit Farm down to the ground, which is going to bring down the rationing credits of every single Panna in Society for months?

And caused three brave Firefighters to have smoke inhalation? And acute burns to Panna Castle Mattea, who was kind to you? How are *your* burns?"

The Doctor smacked the arm which the Medical Assistant Klon had just loosely bandaged. Rubric winced, but she still didn't answer any questions.

"You'll be happy to know that we sent all the remaining Klons from Sweet Fruit Farm for treatment since we couldn't know which of them were involved in your nefarious scheme. I hope it makes you feel good to be responsible for that."

Rubric did feel a horrible pang for those Klons, but she shrugged and said, "You did it, not me. I think you're confused about what the word responsible means."

"So you admit you started the fire? Good. Did you also kill seven people in Velvet City?"

"I certainly didn't."

"I see. So you admit everything else. Good."

Rubric vowed to keep her mouth shut.

The Doctor questioned her further, and the Klon replaced the plastic cuff that bound her hands. Rubric decided to pay attention to her surroundings instead. Yellow and cream walls, brown rubber linoleum floors. A metal examining table. A cabinet. When she had exhausted all the entertainment value she could from the room, she closed her eyes and thought about Salmon Jo. She wondered if it had been worth it, freeing Gold Eyes and the Picker Klons.

Her reverie was interrupted when the Doctor grabbed her shoulder and marched her out into the hallway. There were moaning sounds coming from somewhere Rubric couldn't identify. Or she was hallucinating. The Doctor opened what looked to be a closet door in a long row of closets. Then she thrust Rubric inside and locked the door.

Okay, it wasn't a closet. It was just the size of a closet. Rubric's eyes slowly adjusted to the darkness. There was even less entertainment value here in this bare room. It occurred to her that the moaning sounds came from other patients/prisoners in other closet rooms. "Hello?" she said loudly, but no one responded.

There was just enough room to sit down, so Rubric did. Weirdly, the first thing she thought about was that awful Klon who had knocked her down and scalded her. Why had she done that? She supposed the Klon didn't trust her motives and thought she would do better on her own. She might even be right. That Doctor's robe could probably get her far. The Klon had no reason to trust any Panna. Maybe the Klon didn't want to go to the Land of the Barbarous Ones. Rubric could scarcely fault her for that. But she could fault her for being so violent and horrible. How could she be the same Jeepie Type as Rubric? Maybe your genes weren't your destiny. Maybe the Klon had lived through unimaginable horrors, and that had warped her. Maybe Rubric had been naive to try to help random Klons just because they were genetically identical.

For the first few hours—or what felt like the first few hours—Rubric felt defiant and proud. No matter what they did to her, it was worth it, to fight for the cause of freedom. But hunger, pain, her bursting bladder, and stiffness from her cuffed arms changed her mind. She had made a huge mistake. She should never have left Salmon Jo behind. She was the most important thing in the whole world to Rubric. How could she have abandoned the girl she loved? If she ever saw her again, she would never leave her side. Rubric didn't want to be a heroine anymore.

As time wore on, Rubric realized she was going to die in here. Then get thrown into the high-heat compost unit, an anonymous body, unremembered, unsung. And for what? Some Klons, whose names she didn't even know. All she wanted was to be with Salmon Jo again. Rubric tried to come up with any believable scenario in which Dream could get past the pairs of Security Klons on every floor without being captured, and rescue her. She couldn't think of any way.

For a long time, she tried not to cry. Then she gave in and wept her heart out.

She had completely lost track of time. She slept and woke, screamed and sang. There was no way to know if it was day or night. She felt like she had been in the room for weeks.

Long after she had given up hoping, the door opened. Light flooded into the tiny room. Rubric blinked. The original Doctor was looking down on her, along with a petite, curly-haired Doctor.

"What do you think went wrong with her?" asked the petite Doctor. "Eights aren't usually so troublesome. Stick some clay or a paintbrush in their hands, and they're happy enough. Must have been some environmental factor."

"I've been running some numbers. I think it was the combination of her and her schatzie, a forty-two. I'm going to make an urgent recommendation that in future, eights and forty-twos never share a dorm or academy. Maybe they should be raised in different cities."

To Rubric, she said, "Get up." But Rubric couldn't see what was in it for her. So they dragged her back to the examination room by her legs. The petite Doctor was surprisingly strong. The Medical Assistant Klon was there, and she began to change Rubric's bandages.

"What do you think?" the first Doctor asked.

"Treatment, without question," the petite Doctor said. "And this girl must spend the rest of her life as a Klon. In a closely supervised assignment where she has no contact with other Klons."

Being a Klon wouldn't be as bad as that closet, Rubric thought. Nothing could be as bad as that closet. Was it possible that she wasn't going to die?

"I wonder..." said the original Doctor, and she pulled out her handheld screen. "There's a Panna here in Lvov who needs a lung transplant. End stage of emphysema. We could take a lung lobe from this one."

Rubric didn't like the sound of this. "I have terrible lungs!" she said. "You don't want them."

The petite Doctor snapped her fingers, and the Medical Assistant Klon hastened to cover Rubric's mouth with duct tape. Now Rubric had to breathe through her nose. She felt like she was going to pass out, and she forced herself to calm down.

"Is your patient Jeepie Type eight? I didn't think we had any Panna eights here in Lvodz."

"No, no, she's a sixty-six. They're always getting emphysema. I personally think we should phase out the sixty-sixes. But the originals of eight and sixty-six were sisters, so this one's lungs should be compatible. Maybe I should just take a lung lobe out of this one right now."

This was bad, very bad.

"Sounds good," said the petite Doctor. "I had completely forgotten that eight and sixty-six are compatible. That's very clever. In fact, I have a sixty-six patient myself, with diabetes and a dicky kidney, that I'm about to start on dialysis. But maybe I should just give her a new kidney since you're opening this one up anyway."

Rubric began to struggle, but the Medical Assistant Klon restrained her.

"Oh, I would certainly do that," the first Doctor said. "Once they go on dialysis they tend to tolerate a transplant less well later on. And we have plenty of kidneys walking around, so why not go straight to transplant?"

"This Klon-to-be can still serve Society with one kidney and most of a lung," the petite Doctor said. "Let's put one of her corneas in the freezer-bank as well. She won't be needing two."

Rubric started thrashing around, so the Medical Assistant Klon strapped her arms and legs to the gurney.

"Although…" the first Doctor said hesitantly. "She's made so much trouble. I would hate if that continued, just because we're too softhearted. And it might take so much treatment to make her a good Klon that she'd be of little utility. Do we really need another drooling, lobotomized Klon to carry things? You know, maybe my patient would benefit most from a double lung transplant. Afterwards this one could still serve Society by being compost."

Rubric began to scream through the duct tape.

"That is probably better," said the petite Doctor. "Klon, prepare her for surgery. Let's go pulse our patients."

As Rubric writhed and fought her bonds, the first Doctor leaned over and hissed in her face, "Good-bye, Rubric."

• 172 •

CHAPTER TWENTY-SIX

Rubric stopped struggling. If these were her last moments of consciousness, she had to reflect.

She no longer felt like a brave martyr to a just cause. She merely felt thicko. But none of that mattered. The only thing that mattered was she would never see Salmon Jo again. Salmon Jo would never even know what became of her. She might wait for her for years, the way Prospect had waited for Dream. But in vain. An image came to her of Salmon Jo, living in a tent by the fence, waiting for her to cross. The snow would come, and then spring, summer, autumn, and winter again. The tent would get old, fall apart. So would Salmon Jo. Rubric truly felt she would be ready to die if she could only see Salmon Jo one last time, and tell her how much she loved her.

The Medical Assistant Klon was bustling around making preparations, sanitizing her hands repeatedly. She cut off Rubric's clothes. She gave her a shot. She swabbed Rubric's abdomen and chest, then covered her torso with a sheet. Rubric could hear her clinking around in parts of the room that she couldn't see from her position, flat on her back on the gurney. The Klon wheeled her down the hall. Rubric counted the light fixtures in the ceiling, wishing the last sights of her life could be more beautiful. The Klon brought her into a brightly lit room that Rubric knew from edfotunement was an operating theater. A tray of shining scalpels and other instruments was the centerpiece of the room, next to some other more mysterious equipment.

Then the Klon did a strange thing. She asked, "Did the Doctor say your name was Rubric?"

Rubric nodded. The Klon had short fuzzy blond hair and a round face. She had crinkly lines around her eyes. Rubric bet she smiled a lot. She wasn't smiling now. This was the last face Rubric would ever see.

"That's an unusual name. Did you live in Mountain City, in Yellow Dorm at Masaryka Academy?"

She nodded again.

"Oh dear," the Klon said. She looked disturbed. Then she disappeared out of Rubric's view.

That was too much for Rubric. She began to thrash and grunt as loud as she could through the tape. Finally, the Klon reappeared.

"Oh dear," she said again. "What to do, what to do."

Rubric kept grunting, and finally, the Klon addressed her directly again. "You see, dear, my schatzie was a Nanny Klon in your dorm. I've heard all about you, from her missives. She said you were her favorite."

Rubric grunted even louder. Finally the Klon took off the tape.

"Are you Shine?" Rubric asked hoarsely.

"Oh dear," the Klon said. "Yes, I am."

"Will you help me?"

"I must say, I've never seen a Panna as an organ donor before. It makes me think it must be true that we're all the same, if they can just decide to redistribute you. It'll be hard to tell Bloom that I helped redistribute her favorite young Panna." Then her face hardened, and she said, "But if it wasn't for you, Bloom wouldn't be sweeping the streets now."

"I didn't mean to make problems for Bloom," Rubric said. "I loved her."

"That's all right, dear. You're certainly paying for it now. Getting your just deserts. Can you imagine, a talented Nanny Klon like her, now a Street Sweeper Klon? At first, they just transferred her to an academy in Soot City. But she couldn't stop thinking about the things you said. Before long, they said she was no good at her job, and she couldn't work with young Pannas anymore."

"Please, help me," Rubric whispered. "Please."

"Rubric, if I helped every sad case I saw, I would be lying on one of those gurneys. You have no idea."

It was hopeless.

But then Shine deliberately overturned the entire instrument tray. "Oops," she said, as the glittering instruments hit the floor with a crash.

Just then, the petite Doctor opened the door. "The anesthesiologist is ready to—What's going on in here?"

"I'm so sorry, Doctor. I knocked this over."

"You're terribly clumsy. All Klons are thickos."

"Yes, Doctor."

"Bring me a new tray of sterile instruments," the Doctor ordered. "And don't go flipping any more trays."

The Doctor remained in the room, out of Rubric's sight, after Shine left. Rubric tried to send a mental pulse message of love to Salmon Jo. Maybe Salmon Jo would somehow feel something.

"What's taking that damn Klon so long?" the Doctor said. She left the room too.

Rubric did not know how much longer she lay on the gurney, thinking about Salmon Jo. She didn't think her thought pulses were getting through. Love was just a dream, and death was the only reality. She didn't even deserve to see Salmon Jo one last time. It was better this way. Salmon Jo would find a new schatzie. The important thing was Salmon Jo would survive, and live a happy life.

The next person who came into the room was the last person she expected.

"Rubric, you are no end of trouble," Panna Stencil Pavlina said. "Sometimes, I think you have no sense at all."

Chapter Twenty-seven

R ubric couldn't understand what was going on.
Stencil Pavlina's dialogue with the Doctor, in which Stencil Pavlina repeatedly vouched for Rubric and promised to take responsibility for her, made no sense.

"And I want her with all her kidneys," Stencil Pavlina insisted.

It wasn't until Shine came in and jabbed something into Rubric's abdomen—sure, what was a little more pain?—and said, "Congratulations, you're one of us," that Rubric understood.

She had been chipped and was now a Klon.

A Klon who was not an organ donor. Stencil Pavlina's Klon.

Shine gave Rubric an ill-fitting pair of leggings and a tunic, and Rubric was released. She followed Stencil Pavlina out of the hospital, dazed.

"I must say, I expected a little more gratitude for saving your life," Stencil Pavlina said, as they got into a tiny, hot-pink electric vehicle.

"I am grateful," Rubric said. "Very, very grateful. Thank you so much. It's just that I'm a little disoriented."

Her words rang hollow. In fact, Rubric was not grateful to Stencil Pavlina. She *was* grateful to be alive. She couldn't believe how delicious the autumn air smelled, with a crisp snap of winter in it. She was happy, even, to feel pain all over her body. But somehow her gratitude was not directed toward Stencil Pavlina. Her miraculous rescue seemed more cosmic than that, not something she could ascribe to any one entity. Especially not an entity like Stencil Pavlina.

"I can well understand you'd be disoriented," Stencil Pavlina said. "You've been in there for two days. And you very much smell like it."

"Two days? Really?" It had seemed like much longer.

"Really."

"Stencil Pavlina, I haven't eaten since..." Rubric wasn't even sure. "Can we stop for some food first?"

They stopped at the very same Comfort Station in downtown Lvodz where Rubric had changed into her phony Doctor's robe. That was the last time she had eaten, Rubric realized. The toast was the best thing she'd ever eaten in her entire life. It was soft and hot and exploded with butteriness in her mouth. She almost cried. She gulped down three cups of tea before Stencil Pavlina even took a sip of hers.

"Can you please explain what happened?" she asked Stencil Pavlina. "How is it that you're here?"

Stencil Pavlina was buttering her toast so that the butter was spread perfectly evenly. Rubric did that too, ordinarily.

"I received a pulse from someone who claimed to be a Klon who is our Jeepie Similar."

Dream.

"It said you had been captured by Doctors, and if I had any soul at all, I would do something to help you. Rather melodramatic, or so I thought. I had nothing else to do—inspiration has been failing me of late—and so I began to make some calls. After speaking to a shocking number of people, I did learn you had been taken for treatment here in Lvodz. And so I set out. I do think it is only fair and just for you to become a Klon, after everything you've done. But it is rather going too far to harvest your organs and then compost you. A truly bureaucratic frame of mind came up with that. No imagination, no flair. At incredible expense of spirit and rationing credits, I was able to secure you for my own, on a number of conditions."

"Why?" Rubric asked.

"Why conditions or—"

"Why did you do this?"

"Oh, Rubric, exasperating as you are, I do care for you very much. It may irritate you to hear this, but you remind me so much of myself at your age: talented, rudderless, confused, susceptible to freakish ideas from others, prey to your overdeveloped sense of justice, unable to divine the purpose of life. We all get into scrapes, dear Rubric, but we don't all destroy property. I have also always been fond of a good fire, but contained in a woodstove."

"Stencil Pavlina, what exactly did they tell you? Everything happened because I found out that humans and Klons are the same! We saw it on a spreadsheet, and—"

Panna Stencil Pavlina interrupted her.

"Most Pannas who are smart sense what you and your schatzie had to learn from a spreadsheet. The Klons are not human, because we say they're not. It's a construct. But constructs can be real. The experience of being a Klon makes them what they are, Klons."

Rubric wanted to tell her what scheiss she was talking, but Stencil Pavlina had saved her life less than an hour ago. She looked down at her plate.

"A sulky Klon is even more unappealing than a sulky young Panna. Let me tell you the terms of your release to me. I had to pay half my rationing credits for the next seven years. We'll be wearing out-of-style clothes and eating awful chazarai like this! No more swan-shaped ice cubes for me. If you disappear or set fires or make trouble, those credits are gone down the toilet for nothing. I also had to give both those Doctors a hefty bribe. So, right now, I am very poor. But it would have broken my heart if you had been composted. I am trusting you."

"All right, Stencil Pavlina," Rubric murmured. She really was touched that Stencil Pavlina had sacrificed so much to help her.

In the car again, Stencil Pavlina said, "You do understand that I don't really consider you my Klon, Rubric. That was the only way I could get you out."

"Thank you," Rubric said again.

"Of course, I don't know how to cook or clean, and I've had to de-acquisition the Gerdas because I can't afford them anymore. So I'll be expecting you to help out around the place. But, naturally, the main thing you'll be doing is making art."

"Really?" It sounded too good to be true.

"Absolutely. I'm going to put you right to work. You'll start the moment we get home, which will be late tonight, or early tomorrow morning, depending on how you look at it. This little tin can only goes forty klicks an hour. Unlike the vans you've been stealing. You can start brainstorming during the ride, in fact. I want to have a big show in the late spring. It will blow everyone away! Some people mock me because I haven't made anything new in so long. But that's all going to change, and people will be stunned. I know you can do it, Rubric."

Rubric understood now. She would make the art, and Stencil Pavlina would take the credit. So what? There were worse things.

"You see, Rubric, Klons have no souls, so all your creativity belongs to me."

"That sounds fine with me," Rubric said. "It's a fair deal."

Rubric certainly didn't feel like she had a soul anymore.

Chapter Twenty-eight

That night, Rubric and Stencil Pavlina stopped at another Comfort Station.

"Your stench is overpowering," Stencil Pavlina told her. "I want you to wash yourself thoroughly. I'm too tired to drive through the night, anyway. I'm getting a headache."

First of all, they had more tea and toast. *Who Shall Be My Schatzie?* was playing on the screen. Rubric was riveted. She couldn't believe it was the same season that had been on before all this trouble started, before she and Salmon Jo had fled. Everything seemed so dreamlike now to Rubric, that the drama on the screen seemed more real than her own life. It was the antepenultimate episode, in which this season's heroine had to choose between two bewitching Pannas, who both loved her truly. Next week, her choice would be revealed, and the last episode would show the key-exchanging ceremony. The new schatzies would wear exquisite gowns and crowns of myrtle as they pledged their love for each other and received the keys to their new shared home. Rubric used to daydream about having a key-exchanging ceremony with Salmon Jo one day, but that was clearly impossible now.

Even better than the food and the edfotunement was the shower Rubric took in the overnight room. She turned the water as hot as it could possibly go, until the bathroom filled with clouds of steam and her skin began to turn red. She felt as though all her experiences were being washed away. It was so luxurious to scrub at her skin with the soapy loofah, one of the many small niceties that didn't exist in the Land of the Barbarous Ones. Rubric pictured herself becoming a brand-new person with every invisible cell of dead skin that she exfoliated. At Stencil Pavlina's, she could take showers all the time. Finally, Rubric began to feel faint, and she had to sit down, cradling her head on her knees as the water pounded on her back. She fingered the sore place on her belly where she had been chipped. If Salmon Jo were here, she would give a highly technical explanation of why Rubric felt lightheaded, something about capillaries or that kind of thing. Better not to think about Salmon Jo. By the time Rubric got out of the shower, Stencil Pavlina was snoring in her cot.

The decadence continued as Rubric crawled into her own cot. When had she last slept in a real bed, rather than on cold ground? Rubric reassured herself that even Klons were allowed to sleep in beds. Some light housekeeping would be way easier than the labor she'd done in the Land of the Barbarous Ones. Plus, she'd never have to set eyes on a Cretinous Male or a pregnant woman. Materially, she'd be much better off.

But it wasn't enough. Rubric wanted desperately to believe that beds and hot showers were all she needed, all she wanted out of life. But she found hot tears leaking out of her eyes and pooling on the pillow as she thought about what she really needed. She swallowed back her tears so loudly she was afraid it would rouse Stencil Pavlina.

I can't stay, Rubric realized. *I can't do this.*

Rubric decided to wait just a little longer, to be sure Stencil Pavlina was deeply asleep. Rubric must have fallen asleep while she was waiting, though, because when her eyes suddenly snapped open, the moon had risen. Moonlight was shining into the window.

It felt like her very bones were tired. Rubric considered getting just a little more sleep, or even staying a few days at

Stencil Pavlina's, to give herself a chance to build herself up. But she knew it was now or never. It was so hard to sit up in bed and swing her bare feet out from the warm covers and onto the cold floor.

Stencil Pavlina rolled over restlessly in her cot as Rubric was rooting through her neatly folded tunic for the key to the pink vehicle. That scared Rubric so much that, as soon as she found the key, she crept out of the room, without even trying to find her shoes and stockings.

The night remained still and quiet as Rubric let herself into the pink car and started it up. Good thing electric motors were so quiet. Rubric was a little worried that she didn't feel even a moment's remorse for betraying Stencil Pavlina immediately after she had saved her life. Did feeling remorse over not feeling remorse count?

Rubric only drove a few miles before a terrible thought hit her like an icy wave in the face. She was chipped now! She had to get that chip out, or she would be caught immediately. What was she doing, worrying about an ethical dilemma when she had a Klon chip in her abdomen?

Rubric passed a lake surrounded by reeds. A sign told her it was Wenceslah Lake. She pulled over. There had to be something sharp in this vehicle. Probably Stencil Pavlina carried a precision art knife at all times and she could have taken it if she had thought of it. Rubric berated herself for being so thicko.

At last, Rubric found a flashlight-shaped tool labeled *Window Punch Seatbelt Cutter*. She supposed it was for if you got in an accident and were trapped in the car. There was a retractable pointy bit. Rubric reclined the seat and pulled up her tunic. She took a deep breath. She hadn't even been able to *watch* the Klons cut out their chips. How was she supposed to do this?

"No choice," she muttered.

In a way, it wasn't as bad as she had feared, once she finally got up the nerve to cut herself. Her chip had been placed just that day. All she had to do was reopen the wound the Medical Assistant

Klon had made, and the chip revealed itself. She remembered the other Klons, digging around in their bloody wounds trying to find the chip. It hurt, but nothing compared to crossing the fence. Rubric climbed out of the vehicle, clutching the slick chip. The lake was blue in the moonlight, and the moon was reflected in the center. Just a little dizzy, she threw the chip into the lake. Maybe they would think Rubric had jumped in and drowned. And then driven off in the pink car?

There was blood all over the seat, but Rubric paid it no mind. She hadn't known that she had this icy core inside her, that she was the kind of person who could betray someone and then perform surgery on herself without flinching. Rubric realized she had learned something from Panna Stencil Pavlina, after all. She could be as mercenary as her Jeepie Similar if she had to be.

❖

It was still dark when Rubric reached the wall.

When she realized she had brought nothing to help her climb the wall, she cried. She just couldn't do it alone. Cut all the seatbelts and tie them together? Too short. Hopeless. She had made it this far, but she was totally screwed. Salmon Jo would never even know how close she had come, how much she wanted to get back to her.

As dawn broke, she lifted her tear-stained face from the steering wheel and gazed out at the rosy horizon. As if in a dream, Rubric saw an object rising into the sky. It was shaped like a lightbulb. The light was behind it, so it was just a dark silhouette. It was either getting bigger or coming closer.

The object stopped climbing higher and hung in the sky. Then it floated closer. Rubric caught her breath as she realized what it was. A hot-air balloon.

The balloon was ungainly but beautiful. As the dawn grew brighter, Rubric could see that it was tethered to the ground in some way, on the Barbarous side of the fence. But the balloon was drifting purposefully over the fence. Sparks flashed from the tether where it intersected the fence. Now it was on Rubric's side of the fence, and on Rubric's side of the wall. Rubric started the car and drove toward the spot where the balloon hovered, bumping along slowly over the uneven ground. The tiny electric car wasn't made to be an off-road vehicle, and the noise of rocks hitting the undercarriage was tremendous. Rubric didn't care. Now she could see that ropes with sandbags attached were keeping the balloon in a stable position.

A profusion of ropes, like a net, covered the top of the balloon, and from these hung strong cords that were attached to a wicker basket. The basket was a little smaller than the electric car Rubric had just left. From the basket hung two things. First, a big sheet with KLONS ARE HUMAN written on it and a badly drawn picture of a five-legged dog. Second, a rope ladder dragging a sandbag along the ground. The ladder bobbed up and down, swaying in the wind. A skinny figure clung to the ladder. Climbing down.

"Salmon Jo!" Rubric whispered. She drove as close to the ladder as she could. Jumping out, she left the car running and the door open. She scrambled over rocks and grabbed at the bottom of the ladder as it swayed in her face, whipping just out reach. Looking up, Rubric could see Salmon Jo clinging to the rungs about halfway down.

A huge gust of wind brought the ladder closer. Rubric caught it and began to climb.

The ascent was terrifying. The ladder twisted and tilted. But Rubric had maxed out on being scared. The only important thing was her shaking hands grasping higher rungs. The rope felt funny on her bare feet. She didn't look down. She didn't look up. Just when she was wondering how it was possible to climb so far, she touched the rough side of the basket.

"You're almost there!" It was Salmon Jo's voice. Was Rubric still climbing? She couldn't even tell. She felt strong hands grabbing her arms. She was at the top, and here were Salmon Jo and Dream, hauling her into the basket.

Rubric couldn't believe she was really holding Salmon Jo's warm, strong hand.

Dream was babbling, "Ru, I'm so glad you're okay! Salmon Jo almost killed me when she heard what happened. She shamed all of Hot Buttered Toast Town into working around the clock to make the balloon."

There was more, but Rubric wasn't listening. She took Salmon Jo into her arms and wrapped her arms around her waist.

"I'm so sorry," she tried to say, but Salmon Jo's kisses didn't let her speak. Finally, Salmon Jo tilted her head back so she could look at Rubric's face and stroke her cheek. Rubric couldn't stop shaking. Her heart was pounding, and she could feel blood singing through every part of her body. Her face was strangely hot. She realized the heat was coming from the balloon above and so was the rushing sound in her ears.

"You're bleeding!" Salmon Jo said. "What happened?"

"I'm fine," Rubric said. "It's like nothing. I can't believe you built a balloon."

Salmon Jo grinned, the characteristic twisty smile Rubric loved. "Sorry there's no swimming pool."

Rubric laughed and tried to smack Salmon Jo. But she was gripping Rubric too tightly.

Salmon Jo's face turned serious. "Oh, I was so afraid I'd never see you again," Salmon Jo said. "We were going to come find you."

"I missed you so much," Rubric said. "I'll never leave you anymore. I promise. We'll be together like an undying chain of myrtle leaves. I don't care where I live as long as I'm with you. I'll live with the thicko Barbarous Ones forever, if you want."

Salmon Jo grinned widely. "No reason you have to. We can go anywhere," Salmon Jo said, gesturing at the silky balloon that billowed above them. "It's a big world."

About the Author

Nora Olsen was born and raised in New York City. She received a B.A. from Brown University. Although her mother, a prize-winning author, warned her not to become a writer, Nora didn't listen. Nora's debut novel *The End: Five Queer Kids Save The World* was published in 2010. *Swans & Klons* is her second YA novel. Her short fiction has appeared in *Collective Fallout* and the anthology *Heiresses of Russ 2011: The Year's Best Lesbian Speculative Fiction*. Nora's goal is to write thrilling stories and novels that LGBTQ teens can see themselves reflected in.

Nora lives in New York's Hudson Valley with her girlfriend, writer Áine Ní Cheallaigh, and their two adorable cats. When not writing, Nora works as a babysitter. She also enjoys volunteering for Room to Write, an organization of publishing professionals and writers who visit NYC classrooms to teach creative writing. The highlight of Nora's year is volunteering at Camp Jabberwocky, a summer camp for children and adults with disabilities.

Her favorite writing songs are "Shadow Stabbing" by Cake and "Every Day I Write The Book" by Elvis Costello.

Soliloquy Titles From Bold Strokes Books

Kings of Ruin by Sam Cameron. High school student Danny Kelly and loner Kevin Clark must team up to defeat a top-secret alien intelligence that likes to wreak havoc with fiery car, truck, and train accidents. (978-1-60282-864-3)

Swans & Klons by Nora Olsen. In a future world where there are no males, sixteen-year-old Rubric and her girlfriend Salmon Jo must fight to survive when everything they believed in turns out to be a lie. (978-1-60282-874-2)

The You Know Who Girls by Annameekee Hesik. As they begin freshman year, Abbey Brooks and her best friend, Kate, pinky swear they'll keep away from the lesbians in Gila High, but Abbey already suspects she's one of those you-know-who girls herself and slowly learns who her true friends really are. (978-1-60282-754-7)

In Stone by Jeremy Jordan King. A young New Yorker is rescued from a hate crime by a mysterious someone who turns out to be more of a something. (978-1-60282-761-5)

Wonderland by David-Matthew Barnes. After her mother's sudden death, Destiny Moore is sent to live with her two gay uncles on Avalon Cove, a mysterious island on which she uncovers a secret place called Wonderland, where love and magic prove to be real. (978-1-60282-788-2)

Another 365 Days by KE Payne. Clemmie Atkins is back, and her life is more complicated than ever! Still madly in love with her girlfriend, Clemmie suddenly finds her life turned upside down with distractions, confessions, and the return of a familiar face... (978-1-60282-775-2)

The Secret of Othello by Sam Cameron. Florida teen detectives Steven and Denny risk their lives to search for a sunken NASA satellite—but under the waves, no one can hear you scream… (978-1-60282-742-4)

Andy Squared by Jennifer Lavoie. Andrew never thought anyone could come between him and his twin sister, Andrea… until Ryder rode into town. (978-1-60282-743-1)

Sara by Greg Herren. A mysterious and beautiful new student at Southern Heights High School stirs things up when students start dying. (978-1-60282-674-8)

Boys of Summer, edited by Steve Berman. Stories of young love and adventure, when the sky's ceiling is a bright blue marvel, when another boy's laughter at the beach can distract from dull summer jobs. (978-1-60282-663-2)

Street Dreams by Tama Wise. Tyson Rua has more than his fair share of problems growing up in New Zealand—he's gay, he's falling in love, and he's run afoul of the local hip-hop crew leader just as he's trying to make it as a graffiti artist. (978-1-60282-650-2)

me@you.com by KE Payne. Is it possible to fall in love with someone you've never met? Imogen Summers thinks so because it's happened to her. (978-1-60282-592-5)

Swimming to Chicago by David-Matthew Barnes. As the lives of the adults around them unravel, high school students Alex and Robby form an unbreakable bond, vowing to do anything to stay together—even if it means leaving everything behind. (978-1-60282-572-7)

365 Days by KE Payne. Life sucks when you're seventeen years old and confused about your sexuality, and the girl of your dreams doesn't even know you exist. Then in walks sexy new emo girl, Hannah Harrison. Clemmie Atkins has exactly 365 days to discover herself, and she's going to have a blast doing it! (978-1-60282-540-6)

Cursebusters! by Julie Smith. Budding psychic Reeno is the most accomplished teenage burglar in California, but one tiny screw-up and poof!—she's sentenced to Bad Girl School. And that isn't even her worst problem. Her sister Haley's dying of an illness no one can diagnose, and now she can't even help. (978-1-60282-559-8)

Who I Am by M.L. Rice. Devin Kelly's senior year is a disaster. She's in a new school in a new town, and the school bully is making her life miserable—but then she meets his sister Melanie and realizes her feelings for her are more than platonic. (978-1-60282-231-3)

Sleeping Angel by Greg Herren. Eric Matthews survives a terrible car accident only to find out everyone in town thinks he's a murderer—and he has to clear his name even though he has no memories of what happened. (978-1-60282-214-6)

Mesmerized by David-Matthew Barnes. Through her close friendship with Brodie and Lance, Serena Albright learns about the many forms of love and finds comfort for the grief and guilt she feels over the brutal death of her older brother, the victim of a hate crime. (978-1-60282-191-0)